THE COVERT CAPTAIN

OR, A MARRIAGE OF EQUALS

JEANNELLE M. FERREIRA

For Sonya, who sang it from ballad to page
and
For my wife, who is gently tolerant of the voices in my head

CHAPTER 1

*H*er head was full of noise; her eyes burned full of smoke. She was shouting as she stood in the stirrups, her voice too small to save any of her men. The lancers came on, and the horses screamed, and the men in the saddles did not have time. She saw Sherbourne go to earth with his sabre broken back at the hilts; she was bleeding herself, where her forearm had turned a lance. In her heart she knew they would never, never get out.

You cannot pretend yourself whole. You never left that road by Genappe; you are back there, dead, dead in a charge with half the Lilywhite Seventh, and so you shall always be. And if a bit of you came back alive to England? You know yourself a coward, Fleming.

"Fleming? Fleming, where the deuce've you got to?"

She bolted up from the sofa, savaging old hurts. The major had shouted, so he was still below; she had time to brush her cheeks with her palms, and finding them damp, to smooth back her queue. She checked her silhouette in the long glass over the chimneypiece, buttoned her frock-coat anew and twitched her cravat.

"Here, Major! Just here." Her voice shook not a jot.

"Come down! Bloody frog bloody porters in bloody Calais have made a muck of the baggage. The campaign chests are well enough, but none of the bloody tack's arrived!"

"Hush, Sherry," said another, a woman. "You won't bring it here from Paris bellowing."

Fleming took the stairs with as much speed as she dared— she had grown unused to marble—and stopped herself clicking her heels before the major, just in time. This was peacetime, and a house deep in the country, and she was a guest.

"All right, Fleming? Look as though you're about to cast up your accounts."

The lady at Sherbourne's side hit him, right out, with her knuckles and not her fan. She was not young, perhaps, but none of them were young. She was dressed very *comme il faut*, in white lawn with a sash of periwinkle, with a matched fillet to hold her dark curls from her forehead; but her shoes were frankly worn at the toes, and she had a sensible face.

"Fleming, may I present my sister, the Lady Harriet."

Fleming bowed low and kissed the proffered hand, rising to find the other woman's expression had gone opaque. *She knows. I'm caught out. She must know. Nonsense. Jesus.*

"And Harriet, this is Captain Nathaniel Fleming, with me in the Seventh since…since a damn long time ago, anyway."

"Welcome home, sir," said Sherbourne's sister.

SOMEONE ALREADY RUSTLED the morning papers, and the scent of boiled coffee had begun to lose its edge. It was only half eight—a blistering hour to stand in one's clothes, in peacetime—but the major was mad for the hunt, and had tried to rouse his captain an hour before. It was queer to move through a house so very quiet, so surrounded from every window by trees, and lawns, and the distant crash of the sea. Fleming felt out of sorts and alone, with a turnout of frock coat and breeches instead of regimentals, breathing in the homely smells of English food and English furniture-polish. She loitered outside the breakfast room, not quite pacing, neither advancing; she could not yet shake herself into the part of plain Nathaniel Fleming, gentleman's son, all out of wars to fight and peace to keep. She touched for the hilt of her sabre three times before she quite knew it was no longer there.

It was hunger kicked her over the threshold; Fleming gave a

moment's heed to her tailoring, smoothed her waistcoat, made her back straight and lifted her chin.

"Give you good morning, Sherry," said the captain, and made the best of it.

It was not Sherbourne behind the *Observer.* "Belinda, stay, please, so that Captain Fleming may breakfast."

"I have no wish to be *de trop*, Lady Harriet," Fleming halted, cringing as the downstairs girl dropped the kedgeree spoon on the carpet.

"My brother called you here to shove us together like bundling cottagers, so you are most decidedly *de trop*, but he is off torturing birds at the end of a gun; so the duty is mine to invite you to breakfast. Unless you prefer to take pie and porter and seek him in the grounds?"

To all this Fleming said nothing, only took up a cold roll and the marmalade knife.

"Lord Sherbourne thinks me too decorative to notice a plot against my freedom, Captain Fleming, but I have had the measure of this since he told me his wounded war dog—"

"I beg your pardon, lady, but I am cluttering your country house because I have—at present—nowhere else to go. As for your freedom, I have no designs on it. As for your brother, I believe he appraises you 'deuced clever.'"

"You are under a mistake, Captain. My father did not require cleverness of his daughters."

A quick, queer twist of Fleming's countenance startled Harriet; she forgot to retreat behind the paper. Before she could speak again, the report of fowling shot made the mirrors and platters tremble.

The captain's shoulders hunched. "Your servant, madam," muttered Fleming, and fled the room.

CHAPTER 2

"*I* must beg a truce of you, Captain Fleming."

Bagatelle in A minor broke off with a *sproink* of keys; the captain scrambled to bow. "My lady?" He cast a look to the corridor, sending careful copies of Mr. van Beethoven under the instrument, over Harriet's feet. She had not meant to go creeping—not precisely—but he had seemed to her so intent on his music, from his fingertips on the ivory keys to the toe of his boot keeping time, that for some time she had not wished to draw attention.

"My cousin arrives this evening. It is your fault, and I require an ally."

"…Madam?"

"As you have quite sensibly refused to go grousing, Sherbourne has sent for Viscount Beauchamp. I am thus afflicted with his wife, cousin Dorcas Beauchamp: fickle, fecund, and feeble of wit."

"I am ever at your service, my lady, but I cannot make small talk, or draw, or cheat at cards."

"Bother cards. I want the pianoforte, so I needn't hear her speak. Motherhood is her life! Ah, the happy home! She has seven living children, do you know? And if she'd gotten any of them by her husband, she'd be locked up with the French disease."

The captain colored, coughed, and stooped to gather his music.

"It shan't be onerous. She never rises before eleven."

"But the seven children?"

"All at home in Town, Captain, with the governess!"

"I see." He still coughed, perhaps on the dust of the room, as he endeavored to make his face straight. "I will play for you gladly, so long as the major…"

"Never mind Sherbourne. He goes in fear I shall murder cousin Beauchamp in the cow-pond, as I have threatened since before our coming out. And—and I shall tell him to beat the bounds for his silly grouse, if the shooting troubles you so near."

"It is kindly said, my lady, but a soldier should not fear a fowling piece." The expression upon the captain's face might have been, in a younger man, a grin, but it never reached his eyes, or the lines about them. Without comment as without rudeness, he stepped round Harriet and bowed, leaving the stacked music, the shut pianoforte, and a sheet from the *Contredanses* still under Harriet's slipper.

She did not see him again until the bell had rung for dinner. Looking at him then, in company with her brother Sherbourne, the bilious Viscount, and the centerpiece festooned with one of the day's trophies, it was easier to see how the captain might fade from a room. His regimentals were new and bright, but he was not so tall by a head as Sherbourne, nor a quarter as broad as the Viscount. Because her cousin dropped her fan for him, Harriet knew him handsome enough; but she would not have called it quite that, though his fair queue was smoothly drawn and not so silver-tipped as Sherry's, and his face was—well, it was. Sherbourne had gone into the *tableau vivant* of the affable officer, pumping the Viscount's hand and drawing him along to the table, and Captain Fleming was quiet as ever.

"Come then, old Spaniel, no one's going to bite you; and if they do, you have ranking officer's leave to bite back! Beauchamp, let me acquaint you Captain Nathaniel Fleming of the seventh Hussars, an excellent honorable fellow. Captain Fleming, my very dear cousin, the Viscountess Beauchamp…"

There were war stories enough, though Viscount

Beauchamp had been as far from the Peninsula as decency let him get, that Harriet did not hear the captain speak until well into the entremets.

"I was not there, I'm afraid. I was still mucking about in a field hospital in 'sixteen, and that was a dashed hungry winter."

Dorcas Beauchamp looked up from her dacquoise as though the captain had not said *hungry*, but *spotted pink*. "Captain! Surely there was enough for the ranking men to eat!"

Fleming cleared his throat. "It is an officer's duty to look to his enlisted men. Do you not think so?"

"Oh! I am sure it is as you say, Captain, but dear Beauchamp never wrote a word to me of hunger!"

"Captain, please, spare our coz the pangs of *do you think so*." Harriet was seated just across him, close by Sherbourne at the head of the table, but only five dined, and all could hear it. "No one is hungry now, thank God, and we have had nearly enough of history for one night."

"Nearly enough, madam?"

"You must favor us, first, with why Sherry calls you *Spaniel*, of all things."

The captain shrugged forward, the curls of his queue nearly skirting his chocolate-bowl. "I misremember, madam. I suppose because I kept watch upon the wounded."

"It was only *Thaniel*, at first," Sherbourne said. "Deuced hard to bellow the whole name out in a firefight. It was Spaniel when he set his teeth in and would not let me die."

"Heavens, Major," replied the Viscountess. "You must tell us *that*, and from the beginning!"

Sherbourne went on, obliging his audience, as Fleming grew fascinated with the napery. "You know, my dear, it is the task of the cavalry to charge a line of men until it breaks. There are times… Good men, and brave beasts, find themselves too deep in the line to come safely back."

The Viscountess Beauchamp gasped aloud, but Lady Harriet was straight and set-lipped, white as though Death had touched her on the hand.

"It was only a charge gone badly, dearest, not a six-pound ball in my lap. It was not worth troubling you by the post."

"Sherbourne," said Harriet, not in acquiescence.

"Well. With God's grace and Fleming's, no one came to very much harm."

HER HANDS WERE CRAMPED and sweated round the embroidery frame, and under Harriet's cap her curls lay draggled. Her cousin was dozing, from warmth and shandy, and the Viscountess' girl was blind-busy with a sea of the seven children's mending; the afternoon was bright, the heavens unmarred blue. Harriet nudged the window wide, and leant out.

Horses enough came up the looping gravel drive at Bournebrook, when her brother the Earl was at home, that Harriet no longer remarked their hooves' noise, but on a sudden there was such a crunching and a clatter that she gave a glance below.

"Captain Fleming, what on earth!"

"Your brother Sherbourne, madam!" The captain called up to the window. "Has bought—himself—a hunter!" The horse was black as the devil, gleaming with exertion. Captain Fleming was hatless, and his hands were bound up in the reins, but he sketched a courtesy and beamed a smile. Then he was gone, his coat flying behind as the horse leaped the carriage-drive, turned the corner, and—supposed Harriet—went at a tear for the kitchen garden. A moment later he was back, near standing in the stirrups as the horse paused, then reared up sharpish as if at Harriet's sight.

"Has he bought another uncontrollable horse?"

"No, my lady," Fleming replied, in as courteous a shout as possible. "Now then, my boy, my boy!"

The stallion's front legs crashed down, and the rear flew up. Harriet shut her eyes and braced for Fleming's fall.

"If the beast cannot be controlled—"

"One is endeavoring to so do, madam!"

"But he is *running away*, Captain!" She shouted to the captain's back as the horse gamboled, then wheeled, and flew.

"…only running," drifted up to the window. Harriet saw the captain flatten down in the saddle, to miss the lowest limb of Bournebrook's sentinel oak. Then they were away in earnest, into the fields and out of sight.

"Harriet Georgiana, what are you doing? Hanging from that window like a charwoman!"

"It was so dreadful close, cousin. I felt I must breathe a moment."

"He is rather pleasant, is he not? With those cavalry shoulders, and eyes a very gentian. But only think what his pension must be, dear cousin, if he is compelled to horse-break for Sherry."

"I cannot think—dear cousin—that his pension is any of my concern. I do not believe he draws one. Sherry does not."

"Sherry is not a third son, or a captain, on half-pay." The Viscountess returned to her needlework with a smile that might have dripped goose-grease. "You are twenty-six now, I think?"

"Twenty-eight, coz dear."

"You have left it rather late. Sherry indulges you, letting you sit so on the shelf—but even you might do better than a Waterloo Medal, and a tarnished one at that."

"Dear Dorcas, you must have forgotten; Brother Sherbourne indulges me, as you say, but I have only two hundred pounds a year."

"You have one other commodity, I hope."

"Thank you, cousin. I dare say you will find the room a touch less warm without me," Harriet said, and brought the window sharply shut.

She went out into the grounds with cheeks still flaming, still in spencer and slippers and pinner-cap; she was over the wicket gate and half across the first field before she felt the wet grass against her feet. Harriet cursed aloud and flung the useless shoes over the stile.

"Come now, eternal damnation for old slippers?"

She gave a ridiculous scream and something like a hop. The captain leant against one of the great oaks nearest, the murder-horse's reins thrown over his shoulders, and the beast quite still at his side. He peeled an old apple with a clasp-knife and fed slices to the horse. When the apple was gone, he closed the knife and put it away, scratched the horse along the withers and then said, finally, "My lady."

"The horse," answered Harriet, taking a step away.

"Oh, he and I have reached a gentleman's understanding,"

Captain Fleming said. "It rests chiefly upon apples. Shall you come riding?"

"And be killed!"

Fleming put his head on one side, as the horse might, and his look was half puzzled, half grave. "He will bear two as easily as the wind might bear a leaf, and I will not see you hurt. I am sorry—I would walk him for you as long as you wished, but he is not broken to a lady's saddle. If you are fond of hacking, I will try to use him to it."

Harriet laughed. "What, sitting aside?"

"You might be broken to sitting astride, I gue—" Fleming's hand flew to cover his mouth. He strangled a moment, and colored up to the hair.

Harriet ventured a timid length toward the horse. "He is very beautiful. But I cannot believe he is gentle."

"Stay there; wait." Fleming ducked under the horse's neck, casting the reins back into place as he did so. He put his foot in the stirrup and swung to mount, seemed to rock a moment in the saddle so that its weight moved over the stallion's left flank, and—most terribly high off the ground —dropped his left foot from the stirrup and tucked his right calf close by the left stirrup-strap as a lady might. He sat facing Harriet, aside, and then he patted the horse. It moved —Harriet lost some few steps' ground—and the captain kept his seat. The stallion went a neat ring around Harriet and the oak and then, on a moment, Captain Fleming's boots touched the turf at her side.

"Whirlaway is no trouble, madam."

She laughed again; she must. "What nonsense do you call him?"

"No more nonsense than Sherry called him, upon my word. Black Turk! What a clodding name for such a beast!" Fleming was in the saddle again before Harriet could reply. "Will you come up, or shall I take him back to the grooms?"

Harriet swallowed, wiped her palms dry, and reached up her hands. She had not thought of gloves, either, but she had little enough time to berate herself; she braced her bare foot upon the captain's boot, and then the leather band of his breeches at the knee, and then she was looking down from the warm, rising, falling, ever-moving back of the horse.

"Hold to his mane," Fleming instructed, slipping an arm round her waist, tightly, but as much about his business as a man on the 'Change. "I leave the stirrup to you. We'll have a gallop—a gallop is *easiest*, madam, like pulling a spoon through milk. Be easy," said the captain, either to Whirlaway, or Harriet. "Even should you fall off, it is not so far as it looks."

CHAPTER 3

The captain was a man of his word to Harriet. The pianoforte was kept open hours on end, through all the Schubert they kept at the country house, through a great deal of Mr. van Beethoven from Fleming's campaign chest, and any number of homely broad pieces. Sometimes, when the Viscountess had nothing upon which to discourse over the music, Fleming could be induced to sing. His voice was true, if not ornamented; he knew any ballad Harriet could name, and forty she could not.

At whiles it seemed he forgot the women were in the room. He played from his head or from sheets copied over by hand, kept together by bits of silver braid from a cavalry dolman; they were not titled or marked at all. Harriet turned for him, sometimes, and wondered every moment if he noticed the pages' change.

"That is tiresome," Viscountess Beauchamp said, sharp into an afternoon gone honey-slow, warm, and still. "What nonsense do you give us, Captain?"

"It is true, the cadenza is much better played upon the harp," Fleming said, as if it pained him to move so quickly from music to speech. "As you do not care for *opera buffa*, my lady, I thought to give you tragedy. It is Monsignior Rossini; the one good piece for his Desdemona."

"You give us tragedy surely enough," the Viscountess answered, and Harriet bridled in protest.

"Oh! I thought it lovely."

"Very lovely—words a bit rubbish—I wish you might have seen it, lady Harriet. We had four days' run-off to Naples in 'sixteen, and I dragged Sherry to the theatre by his pelisse."

"May I suppose then, Captain, you understand the Italian tongue? I would not have thought it of an upstart from the West Riding."

"Music has no tongue, my lady Beauchamp," Fleming said with mildness spread thick. "Or else many as the stars. Do you not find that one of its singular joys?"

He had given her cousin the rout, and Harriet knew that would spark to anger; she set her knitting-needles down and crossed to the pianoforte, leaning to raise the key-fall where Fleming had dropped it shut.

"Pray sing, instead," she asked. "Something in English, with words exceeding small."

He did not smile until she did. Then he gathered the music away, shook his wrists and fingers, and struck up again.

"As sweet Polly Oliver lay musing in bed, a sudden strange fancy came into her head; nor father nor mother shall make me false prove—I'll 'list for a soldier and fo—"

The knock upon the doorpost made Harriet quite set her teeth; it was not a ballad she had ever heard. Before she could send away the servant—or stamp her foot—Sherbourne half-bowed himself into the room, his cutaway spangled with ash from forgotten cigarillos, his face mirth all over.

"I mislike to interrupt the musicale, but Spaniel, there's a parcel for you below."

"For me! What on earth!"

"No direction on the thing," Sherbourne shrugged. "Beg you go and see to it. It is rather cumbersome."

Fleming stood, his countenance blank with bafflement. "Pray accept my excuses, my lady Beauchamp, my lady Harriet. Major, you make it sound like a thing alive!"

Sherbourne shrugged again.

"Must I go armed, man?"

It was not the captain's question but the cast of her brother's grin that stirred Harriet. "Captain, do go carefully. Sherry, if you've buttered the staircase again—!"

"Sister, I was *twelve*," Sherbourne protested.

Harriet, lumbered by the viscountess as she was, gained the front door some seconds behind her brother. She was in time to see Captain Fleming leap from the front steps with a heart-stopping shout.

"Malabar!"

There was a horse standing in the drive, with no groom to speak of, a slim-legged dappled grey with four white pasterns and a tail docked short. The tack Harriet recognized; the horse she had never seen. Captain Fleming hung by his arms round the beast's proud neck, laughing.

"Stopped your pining and sighing, have you, Fleming my love?" Sherbourne might have taken a Sunday-school prize and a cone of sweets. His hands were hooked in his Cossack-trousers' pockets, and he beamed like a cherub. "That'll be a deuced relief."

"I thought never to see her again."

"What do you take me for, leaving such a beast to the Frogs!"

"But the fees, Sherry, you know I cannot—" The captain stopped his mouth just in time, as even a third son ought.

"Can't hear you. Talk up next time, Spaniel."

"Sherry, *je t'embrasse!*"

"I should hope not," he answered. "Good God, Spaniel, do you suppose I'd see her badly looked after?"

Fleming unfolded from his crouch by the mare's forefoot. "Do you suppose I'd let you keep a groom who did? Only heaven knows what has befallen her, since we parted; she might have been cold-shod, out there over the Channel."

"*Quelle horreur,*" Sherbourne answered. "I gave that the beast should be shod afresh in Dover, you idiot, by a proper blacksmith. Do you mean to ride or not?"

Fleming broke off gazing like a man in love. He bowed, very low, and then beckoned up to Harriet. "My lady, may I make you acquainted?"

Harriet lingered only for her cousin to wind the *H* of her Christian name. She came down onto the lawn swallowing her fear by degrees, though the horse had lowered its head and was nosing and striking at Fleming's hips as if it would begin to eat him.

"Brazen," said Fleming, exceeding fondly. "I've nothing for you. Get away."

"Wh-what on earth must it want?"

"She," corrected Fleming. "Wants comfits—or candied violets, game girl she is." He remembered himself, and cleared his throat. "This is Malabar out of Bacchante, by Selim; and so, in her way, as great a lady as you."

Harriet said all she could on the matter, which was "Quite," and handed over her comfit-case to Fleming.

"I much doubt she will save you any, if she sees them go to and fro like that."

"Oh! I am at her service, Captain. A lady must have refreshment who has just made the Channel crossing."

The captain gave her a look appraising and admiring all at once. Then he took Harriet's wrist, most delicately, and shook a bright hail of caraway comfits onto her palm. Before she could balk, he had guided her hand right under the mare's nose.

Above them, by the sound, the Viscountess Beauchamp had taken too much snuff.

FLEMING'S light tenor came in from the garden as Harriet sat over the wreck of last week's broadsheets. It was *Green Grow the Rushes-o*, she supposed after a moment, but not as she had heard it ever before.

"Lies our Sherry on the ground, fallen off his mount-o! Lord, but he's a drunken sod, and ever more shall be so!"

"Spaniel, you bastard."

"…said you would hear it," Fleming said, half lost in laughter and the steady jingling of tack. "I pray you don't impugn my poor dead mother; all my wickedness fell from the proper side of the blanket."

They were coming round to the carriage-drive, horses nearly in step, and Harriet died to know what could have made Sherry forego breakfast; she finished the bitter last of her chocolate and hurried to the door, not pausing for Sherry's man to open it for her.

"How beautiful!"

"Martial, sister. A beast of Her Majesty's Hussars is *martial*."

Harriet, hair and waist bright with poppy-colored sateen, came down the great steps to stand at the head of Fleming's grey mare. She reached a hand to the thick plush of the sabretache by Fleming's knee and traced its gilt insignia, casting only half a glance to the rider. "Martial, then. But why get them up like this? Is there a parade in Bournesea?"

"Have to dress 'em up so even in peace, now and again. Keep them used to it." Sherbourne leant across to her from his saddle, clinking and rasping with sabre and musketoon. "Best enjoy the freedom of the place while we've gone. If Beauchamp tires you, have Linton take you out in the carriage."

"May I not accompany you, sirs?" Harriet looked as much to the captain as her brother.

"You may not, Harry. You shouldn't care for ten miles on a beast like this; and how should we bear you? The kit is six stone already."

"I think it should be splendid," she protested.

"Dearest, you would be frightened. Leave gentlemen's business to gentlemen—"

"Ah, Sherry, shuck your pack," said Fleming.

"Not mine, sir! The lunch is in it!" Sherbourne's voice was still amused, but tinged incredulous. He patted the neck of his white gelding. "Besides, this one is stout enough, but not so steady as my Kestrel."

Fleming looked down at Harriet, kindly. He took off his battered hat, and in the sun his queue glinted like a sovereign. He buckled off his sabre and eased it to the ground by Harriet's feet, tossing the hat down beside it; then with both hands he tugged at the straps of his pack. "Six stone," he agreed. "Madam, how many stone have you?"

"Come now, this begins to be unseemly! And we're wasting half the morning. Harry, turn about!"

The captain grinned at her, just a flash and a moment, before Sherbourne cut him off.

"Spaniel, I forbid it. A woman on a war-horse! Will you send the beast mad?"

"Malabar will go steady, Major."

"If you take my sister up in front, Malabar will bear you to hell," said Sherbourne.

"She has done, before," Fleming answered, hardly to hear. He looked again to Harriet, mirth drained away, and ducked his head to her. "Come by, Malabar. Come by, then." Fleming's horse neatly sidestepped Sherbourne's white, and in spite of rider and weapons and gear was fast enough to make Fleming appear a blue-and-white blot at the lawn's edge in a moment.

"I s'll give you *come by*, Captain! Come by indeed, sir!"

CHAPTER 4

There was a scratching at Harriet's sitting-room door. Too regular and quiet for one of Sherry's dogs, and in any case they ought all to be kenneled; too discreet for a servant, and Harriet had not rung. When the noise persisted, she left *Frankenstein* spraddle-backed on the hearthrug and went to the door in her shawl and shift.

"You are waking, then."

Harriet gaped, but to Fleming's relief had sense enough not to cry out. He kept carefully to the corridor side of her threshold, dropped the slide of his lantern to make up for what firelight came from within, and handed over a plain cloth bundle.

"G-give you good evening, Captain. It—it is half three o'clock."

"I was out to the stables late," said Fleming. "I thought you should like to ride, after what passed this morning; I came to see if you would."

"What, now?" Harriet unwound the bundle and something —one boot, another—thumped to the carpet. "Now—and in breeches!"

"You cannot ride properly in a shift, and I beg you give Sherry no reason to blow my brains out in the daylight. So, yes, now."

Harriet sorted the shirt and breeches over in her hands, as if sounding their mysteries out. They were exceeding worn, clean, pressed, smelling somewhat of ambergris. "Five minutes," she said, at last.

"Three," said Fleming, "or I shall tell you how the book ends."

"Captain," cried Harriet in a whisper, "you are no gentleman!"

"At your door in dead of night, and handing you my breeches?"

"Making threat to spoil my new book," replied Harriet, and shut the door against him.

"THAT HORSE IS NAKED!"

"I'm sure she does not think so." Malabar stood under the sentinel oak, dappled silver in the moonlight; there was a pad and a plain groom's saddle on the mare's back, and a plainer cavesson. If it had not gleamed like all the captain's tack, Harriet would have taken it for a rope halter.

"How shall I ride without stirrup or bridle?"

"You have no need of them. Shall I put you up?"

Harriet balked again. "I'll fall right over the other side!"

"If you should, the turf is moderate soft." There was amusement in Fleming's voice, but no mockery. "We have not all the time in the world. Up?"

"How shall I make her go, without ribbons and a bit? I cannot guide a horse with nothing in its mouth."

"You guide her with your legs, same as you hold your seat. I have the ribbons, such they be—" Fleming tugged at the cavesson, very fondly, and the mare swung her head round as if to box Fleming's ears. "A bit you will not have with her, not yet. You pull too much in the turn."

"You have never seen me ride, sir!"

"I have seen your mare's mouth." More gently, Fleming went on, "It is not a fault, it is a fear; you pull because you dread falling off. You are *going* to fall off, I say, aside or astride, and you will keep the fear if you keep your feet on the ground."

Saying so, the captain hoisted Harriet by the elbows and half braced, half shoved at her hip. Harriet gasped and flailed, caught in skirts that were not there, and any moment expected a horrid dizzying drop.

The horse had not bucked her. She was in the saddle, and she clutched at the depths of the warm grey mane for dear life while Fleming, silent and quick, placed his bare hand upon Harriet's knee and calf, and gripped her ankle through the borrowed boot.

"Heels down, eyes up," he said, and ducked under Malabar's head to repeat the whole show upon Harriet's right side. When he had done, he came and eyed her, very critically.

"Madam, do you lace?"

"I beg your pardon, sir! I do not, at three in the morning!" Harriet was near enough to kick him in the head, but she had a great fear of startling the horse. Fleming, unruffled, reached up for something out of her line of sight.

He touched the small of her back, just at the band of the threadbare breeches. A shock, a jolt, a shiver—

"But that is perfect," said Fleming. "Why on earth did you sit there like a pudding? I thought I must borrow Sherry's riding corset."

Her back straight as a whalebone busk, and tingling, Harriet realized he had not meant to touch her at all; he might have touched the mare's back, for all it troubled him.

"Is all well, madam?"

"All's well," she lied.

Fleming heard it. "Malabar will stand for Congreve rockets, if she must. I think she will stand for you. Should you care to walk, hold tight with your knees—get out of her mane! Hold my hand, if you like, and hold to the pommel with the other."

"Hold your hand! Don't be ridiculous, sir, who shall hold the *horse*?"

"You," replied Fleming. "I've no need to pull upon her to make her walk. She will do that at your word, I think."

"You think!" Harriet was beginning to tremble.

"Oh, I have never tried her with anyone but myself. I have not been in the habit of lending Malabar."

"Why take such pains with me?"

"I told you, I thought you should like it. And if you were my —sister, I had rather you learnt to ride properly and stir a scandal than muck about side-saddled and break your neck. Get *up*, Malabar."

Harriet lurched when the horse moved, but did not fall—or

else she fell continually, first one side, then the other, rolled as if amidships with the rolling of the horse.

"This is… this is not so queer as I supposed. I thought cavalry-horses were all savage!"

"Not so queer as you supposed," Fleming laughed, low. Then he went on, "No. Your horse is your weapon, your shield, and your dearest savior; you do not want her savage, or ill-natured. They are let on the field to plunge, and bite, and kick, but those things are for war, not for habit."

"Then Sherry's war gelding is not—not violent?"

"No, to be sure! Why on earth?"

"He has given me a lie these many years! He has always said a war-horse will kill a woman who comes near."

Fleming near doubled over with a sudden cough; the morning dark was chill, and the dew in the air was heavy. "S-stand, Malabar," he wheezed. "Stand!"

"Captain, are you well?"

"Oh," he said, clearing his throat at last. "Oh, I beg your pardon. Sherry—Sherry was putting a garland upon the truth, madam, for your safety. A war-horse is a most dangerous creature, indeed."

"But you have just told me—"

The captain half waved, struggling again with a cough.

"Dangerous for a woman, I mean. Women spook war-horses, you see," he gave it up, pressing his face against the grey mare's withers.

"Surely it is not true. Cousin Beauchamp has been to Wellesley's country-house, and she says any lady who likes may ride him—ride Copenhagen."

The cough grew explosive; the horse was obliged to stand again, and Fleming stamped and buried his mouth in his elbow. He wiped his face upon his cravat before speaking again.

"His Grace the Duke must do what he likes, but I can tell you, that charger is quite mad. Perhaps he likes being rubbed round the ears by great ladies, and fed bread and sugar."

"I don't know, sir. When Wellesley came here to dine, I scarce touched his hand; we only fed him turbot and venison."

"Come," said Captain Fleming, through his door. Short and sharp, but not peremptory as her brother; used to command, accustomed to obedience, but not too much. *And very used to his own devices,* thought Harriet, when she lifted the latch and he neither spoke further, nor glanced up.

He looked almost girlish, when first she saw him. Standing

in his stockings, his coat still clothing the back of a chair, the captain was shorter and more slightly framed than she had thought. He had chosen a plain cravat, not an officer's black stock, and Harriet thought he must have set down his razor only a moment before; no morning trace of beard showed above the linen. His fair hair still fell unbound over his shoulders, and he was absorbed in polishing his boots.

"You must let Linton do that," said Harriet.

Captain Fleming gave a shout. Whatever he had expected, water-boy or fresh coal scuttle, it was not the Major's sister in morning silk and walking shoes. He brought his blacking rag before his face, without thinking; the carbon smell of it screwed his eyes shut, and well-mannered words went by the open window.

"Indeed," she went on, to excuse herself, "I thought your man was with you, at this hour."

"John Linton," said Fleming, not quite recovering himself. "My boots!"

"Yes, if you have no one here to see to it. I am certain Sherry would not mind."

"Good morning, my lady, and thank you, but Cap—*Mister* Linton was my superior officer half across Spain. Thinking him any man's bootblack sends me queer in the head."

"My brother is an excellent master." Harriet said it to her gloves.

"Yes, or he should not be mine." The captain coughed. "And for yourself, my lady Harriet? What would you of me, at eight of a clock?"

"I came to say it is near setting-off time, as Sherry means to walk—leg and all!"

"What, to the hunt?"

"To Bournesea church! It is—it is Sunday, Captain."

He murmured, and seemed contemplating which was the graver sin, to stand before her stocking-footed or, in her presence, to put on his boots; in the end Fleming thrust his hands behind his back.

"Sherry tried to put me off by say—" Harriet colored up. "*Are* you a Dissenter?"

"Nay. No," he amended, and bent again to swipe at a smudge that was not there, as if the heather-edge of the West Riding were a stain to be rubbed out. "No more than my lord the Earl."

"Accompany us, then!"

"As Sherry does not care to suffer alone?" Captain Fleming was, for a moment, unkind.

"As it is a beautiful morning, and I wish it."

He bowed. Then he turned to the soldier's chest at the foot of his bed, and searched in it to his elbows. Harriet would not venture to peer among a man's possessions, but without rising onto her toes she saw black stocks and white shirts—few—laid precisely in the upper tray, books and papers mosaic-close below. The books Captain Fleming wanted did not come easily to hand.

The first was an old Watts hymnal; the second had no gilt left to tell its title. Its Morocco cover was flaking, and the corners were beaten soft. One of the captain's plain black ribbons marked it. The pages stirred, when Fleming tossed the book down to button his coat, and it fell open to *The Order for the Burial of the Dead.*

IN THE CHURCH PORCH, Fleming found himself suddenly possessed of hymnal, mitts, comfit-case, fan, and stunning view of the smirk on Sherbourne's face as Harriet walked ahead.

"You are a pawn, Fleming," Sherbourne laughed, loudly as he dared. "Poor bastard, long may she use you to cock a snook at my cousin. Dozy cow," he added, and then, "Give you g'morning, Vicar!"

It was Fleming's turn to laugh, then, as Sherbourne looked like a boy caught out and Harriet looked a queen.

"Spaniel—Spaniel, I say. Give me that rubbish." Sherbourne gave a hand for his sister's things. "Can't say she's ever been squired of a Sunday. Stopped me doing it ages ago. You're considerable more pleasant in the face, at that."

"M-major?"

"Get *up* there, Captain. It's a lady's elbow, not an infantry square."

"Your sister," tried Fleming.

"My fists, sir!"

Fleming ducked away. The ladies were passing out of the churchyard, even hampered as they were by skirts; he was obliged to trot—to run, most surely—and keep one hand to his Sunday hat lest it fly. He reached the Viscountess' side without too much blowing, and when she halted, he bowed so deeply as to see the flyspecks on her stocking.

"Viscountess Beauchamp. If I may deprive you of my lady Harriet…?"

She did not address him. Harriet gave Fleming a curtsey past his rank, for the Beauchamps' sake, and then tucked her arm under his. Fleming cut his stride only a trifle, and thought they went along well together in parade step; they went on some lengths in quiet before he noted Harriet was blinking, and blinking, and speaking under her breath.

"Madam?"

"Dam' good of you back there, I was only saying," she

answered. "Do you know, Sherry said you would not come to church?"

The captain lost pace for a moment. "In truth, madam, I have not often—since the Brabant—I have grown unconvinced any god is to be found in church."

To his surprise she regarded him steadily, and pressed his arm. "Sherry will not speak of it, but I believe he is much the same. I do not know him as well as I used—I was not much in his confidence while the Seventh was abroad—but I think he will throw the vicar over for whisky soon enough."

Fleming knew her correct, but found that his answer was to keep his lips stitched.

"My father was Colonel of the Regiment, before his wound sent him *hors de combat*; Sherry has been the king's man so long as I've been alive. Men do what they must. I would a thousand times Sherry drink than he shot himself."

"As you say, madam," said Fleming, and meant it.

"You do not really agree." Harriet bent her brows at him. "You have been two weeks with us, and you are all lemonade and chocolate. I do not believe you take even hock. For a godless man, you are quite Methodist."

"Can't stand hock, don't like claret," Fleming answered, nettled to frankness. "Ratafia quite disguises me, and port is damned disgusting. And I do not care for losing my wits."

"What do you do, then? When you must."

"Ballads, madam. Horses." He could not look at her. "Forgive me. I have given you a most melancholic walk."

"Oh, no! We have left the family quite behind, though—or else they are all ahead. I must thank you, Captain, for sparing me two miles 'midst the Beauchamps, and in your turn you will forgive me for bringing the talk to war?"

"There is no need, madam, for pardon or for thanks."

"But I do not like being at evens with you. It bores so." She considered a moment, fiddling with her lily-white Sunday tucker; she let go his arm, and said, "Harry."

"…Madam?"

"My Christian name is Harry." She left him, indeed, on an uneven footing of a sudden. She looked at him for a moment—they did not differ much in stature, and her brown eyes were startling bright—and then swept up her skirts and ran from the road.

In a spate of words unfit for Sunday, or women, or running at speed, he lit after her. He had no good idea through whose field they were racing, or its purpose; Fleming spared a prayer for averting cowpats as he ran. In breeches it was a small thing to overtake her, though they might otherwise have been matched. When she went over a low stone boundary, he was just behind.

"Blast! Bother! Bother!"

Fleming pulled up short to keep from knocking her to the earth. "Harry?" He said before he thought. "Are you well?"

"*Bother.* It's only—I've still beaten you," she wheezed. "It's my bloody walking dress, ruined. Now comes the sermonizing upon footraces on Sunday." Harriet groaned. "Cousin Beauchamp will have raptures." She flopped into a pile of leaves beneath the wall, costume unheeded, and scowled at the petticoat showing through the russet silk.

"My lady, I have always delighted in spiking an enemy gun."

"Sir?"

Fleming took a smart little housewife from a recess of his coat, knelt in the leaves at Harriet's side, and examined the tear. Instead of giving needle and thread to Harriet, he turned the skirt's edge to its wrong face and began mending, with stitches tiny and even and quick. He pleated the repair up into the sunlight and then, inspection over, threaded new silk to the needle and stowed it away again.

"You are ten times keener at that than I," said Harriet.

"One is responsible for one's turnout, madam, and those lovely braid facings are the very devil."

"Ugh, to be called to account for your uniform in the middle of a real war! Sherry always had his batman look to it."

The captain was replacing his gloves; he held up one hand and waved, near shyly.

"Heavens, what would Sherry have done without you?"

"Gone stark naked, madam. He had a proper batman for his firing piece and his boots; I lost my man at Orthez, and never much wanted another."

CHAPTER 5

*S*he skirted the paddock on purpose to find him, and because she had rather spend a quarter hour going uphill to the house than treading her business in Bournesea over with her cousin. Hidden under a new frill, a pair of stockings she did not need, and a sheaf of letter-paper in Harriet's basket were Mr. Polidori's *Vampyre* and two new pens.

Captain Fleming was upon Malabar's back, leading Sherbourne's white war-horse on a longe. He lifted his hat to her as she came past the paddock fence, but turned again to his task with barely a smile; a half-second later the white gelding shied and reared, terribly close to the captain and his mount.

Fleming's voice was cool, almost too low to hear. "*Courbette*, Malabar." Harriet had half a lifetime of French, but was not ready to see the grey mare go straight onto hind-legs, rearing upcurved as the white gelding had, with the captain seated easily as breathing; then Malabar's arc became a rippling leap forward, so that the mare and the gelding came down to the turf together.

"Stay in step, you blockhead!"

The gelding faltered at the command, collided with Malabar's near flank, and on a moment all their tack was in a tangle.

"Go gee, if you've a mind!" Fleming leant out over his mare's bridle, to disengage the gelding's longe-line; the animal's jaw caught Fleming upon the right arm. Then the horse shook free, annoyed, showed his rear shoes and ran.

"Captain?" Harriet was already over the fence. "Captain Fleming!"

He slipped from the saddle limp, without a murmur, fell to the paddock's turf and lay still. When she reached him, his eyes were half-open and he was grey in the face. Malabar stood half over the captain, cairn-solid, head drawn low, sharp-shod hooves pawing when Harriet drew near.

"Please move," she begged, crouching closer. "Oh, please move." She could not have said whether she spoke to horse or rider, and it glanced off both. Upon the ground where Fleming had fallen was something wet, darker far than dew;

red, when Harriet edged her slipper past. She said the worst word she knew.

"Stupid horse," she snapped. Her throat was thickening. "Harry, don't be an ass, *don't* be a girl." Harriet forced herself to look the grey war-horse in the eye. She threw back her shoulders and tried to sound like Fleming. "Whoa, back!"

Malabar retreated.

From the ground at Harriet's elbow, a wheezing sound, a laugh. "That was…very well done."

"You're alive," breathed Harriet, scrambling to aid him to sit.

"Pity." Dazed still, Fleming blinked, and scrubbed his left hand over his eyes. "Wh-where's Mesrour? The white horse. Won't hurt you, but silly enough to… to clear the fence. Too young for the work. Too silly. A pox on your bastard son, madam!"

Harriet sat away from him, afraid he had been struck witless.

"Sorry. Sorry. Was addressing the mare."

"Sir, you are unwell. Let me fetch Sherry to you, or the grooms—"

"No!" On a moment Fleming's voice was distinct. "No. I

beg you don't be foolish. I've broken nothing. It's nothing of consequence."

"You're bleeding." For proof, Harriet turned back the right-hand sleeve of Fleming's barn frock. Blood welled from the edge of a long and wicked scar, seeping along a bruise already crimson.

"I will see to it," said Fleming.

Harriet reached behind, to unfasten the coarse, bloody smock and cast it away. "If you will but let me—"

She might have put a knife into Fleming's back. He leapt upright, though he staggered, and his unhurt arm went over Malabar's neck. "I will see to it!"

"As you wish," Harriet answered. She got herself off the ground, her skirts a soaked riot of red and brown and green. She wished, for her part, that they were not so alike in height; she could match the captain's gaze, and read all she found there.

He flinched. He would not give his back to her, but he could not keep her eye.

"Pray excuse me, Captain." More grieved than nettled, and nettled that she grieved, Harriet swept past him and set about finding a graceful way over the fence.

SHE STOOD with her knees pressed tight to stop them shaking. She had padded Nate's boots out with rags to make herself taller, and laid the knot of his faded black stock to hide the dip where her Adam's-apple was not. The fall-front of the pantaloons she was less sure of, but a cavalryman wore a coverall, or breeches, and a cavalryman she would be. Eleanor did not lean upon Barley, much as she wished to do; she lined her toes up with the gelding's hooves, turned her feet out and clasped her hands behind her back in her brothers' air.

"You're not overgrown," the officer said, and made her jump. He was five years older, perhaps, than she; he had left boyhood behind, but his eyes were wicked and sparking. His black hair was quite curled, and seemed not all to fit under his shako. "Why should you be a cornet and not a curate?"

"One king is very like t'other, and I am passing better with horses than I m'n be with souls."

"Has that tongue in your head been educated, boy?"

"Yes, sir," she said, and stood so straight she must tip backward.

"Then for the Lord's sake speak properly, or I will send your tongue home to Yorkshire and the rest of you to the devil, and you may say Lieutenant Sherbourne sent you. Is that horse yours?"

"Mine, sir, from my father," Eleanor spoke truth. She patted Barley's gleaming side. "John Barleycorn, by Sorceror."

The officer whistled, low. When he had given Eleanor a hand-up, he spent five minutes more going over the sorrel gelding. "That is deuced fine. Very well! Walk your beast."

"My beast comes with me upon him," Eleanor answered.

"He does not, boy, if you do not heed an order. Show me a hand-gallop, and take him round as I say."

Eleanor sat forward, to give herself height in the stirrups, and nudged Barley up to pace as the officer bade; then all she must do was listen, and make Barley heed the—

"Wheel about left! Come by right! Come by left and tight to me, tight I said!"

The officer gave Barley a touch with his crop when they passed, and gave one to Eleanor for good measure. She had expected it; she stayed stuck in, and kept her gaze between the gelding's ears.

"Forequarters light!" The demands resumed, and fast. Eleanor collected her wits against the sting in her leg, dropped her seat and made Barley rear.

"Hindquarters light!"

"What, from a stop?"

"Speak me formal, boy, I don't care who your horse is! Say, from a stop, Lieutenant?"

"Sir, from a stop, Lieutenant?"

"As you must, you silly little sod!"

Past the unflinching young officer at full gallop, she reined tight, clung like a limpet, and did not fly over Barley's head as he showed his hind shoes. It cast up her stomach and rattled her teeth.

"Get down, then. What's your name?"

"N-Nathaniel Fleming, sir."

He offered her his hand, and she endeavored to grip as hard. "Could you do as well upon a big horse, a drum horse? You are small for much save the drum, but we are lately tasked—honored with it."

"I have never been tried," said Eleanor, a tremble rising from throat to voice.

The lieutenant's look was suddenly kind. "I suppose you would rather not part from this one. Well! Don't get him shot from under ye, then, Cornet Fleming."

"Sir?"

"Take your beast to the quartermaster—with you upon him—and say particularly, Lieutenant Sherbourne wonders have we a coverall short and narrow."

Sherbourne's stable-door made a sound like a firing piece in the night. She woke hay-strewn and grievous sore, and hurried upright by the aid of Malabar's foreleg. A prospect agonizing stiff, now, to sleep on a stable floor, no matter how deep the bedding; it queered and sickened her as she came out of the dream. She was, for a moment, still green and young, still Nora, tasting doubt when she lowered her voice and stood to her full height. She thought to duck into the shadows of Malabar's box—it was rather the size of her room in Bournebrook house—and pass the night's watches in what she could call peace.

"Captain Fleming?"

It was not Sherbourne, nor any of the grooms.

"Sherry and Beauchamp are sitting to midnight supper, but I thought you should not wish—Captain Fleming? Hello?"

Fleming let a mash-bag rattle conspicuously, and stepped from Malabar's stall plucking straws out of his shirt. He gave her a smile in greeting's stead, because he did not trust the timbre of his voice.

Harriet, pale in a pale gown, bore a lantern in one hand and a covered pail in the other. Confusion and concern touched her countenance; she looked toward his right arm, bound in a feedsack sling, and nearly scowled.

"That is what you meant by seeing to it, I suppose? You and Sherry are in the same mold. I hope it is decent clean!"

Fleming shrugged. "Clean, yes, and well bound with honey. Malabar thought the first dressing appetizing to a nicety."

Harriet smiled back at him. "I fear she will be spoiled, then, for the baked apples." She offered the pail to Fleming, with linen tucked round to keep the repast warm: three baked apples and a cork-stopped bottle of custard, some slices from the officers' joint of beef, and a loaf of bread. "I have eaten my share already. It leaves two for Malabar, and one for you."

Fleming turned up a camp seat with most of its legs and

canvas, after a moment's searching, but Harriet did not take it, instead wandering the stable while he ate. His tack was hanging, clean, a bit apart from the rest; she touched over it thoughtfully and remarked, "You might have bought colonel twice over."

"Men with no land and no club are not colonels," laughed Fleming. "And yes. It is the terrible vice of my fathers. From birth I breathed the contagion. Malabar I bought with His Majesty's gratuity after Orthez—and a little more besides. Well," he excused himself. "She promised very fine, and I needed a horse."

"She is beautiful, and I should not like to meet her in war," said Harriet. "Is it because she proved so well that Sherry bought her colt?"

"Beg pardon?"

"You said—you called his white war-horse her son."

"So he is." Fleming nodded. "Poor Malabar, to have her heart stolen so by a nameless Frenchman! But Sherry did not buy him—rather I would not have bought him for Sherry, and I have been his man for horse-flesh these many years. Mesrour is strung too high. But Sherry will ever choose an idiot white horse over a dun cob who stays stuck in."

"You made my brother a gift of that horse," said Harriet. "You might have made two hundred guineas in Tattersall's."

"Oh, not so much as all that," Fleming dismissed it. "And Sherry has given that Malabar may board here the rest of her days; call it no gift, but a bargain." With his unencumbered hand he flicked crumbs from the napkin and folded it into the pail, took up the rosy-skinned baked apples, and pitched them gently into Malabar's box. "Two hundred! She eats thirty guineas per annum, apples aside. When we have no errands to run for His Majesty, I cannot afford her."

"You must have died a thousand times, to leave her in France. You speak of her so fondly."

"I did. I am. Fond of her." The captain cleared his throat. "She is as much my friend as Sherry, and has never cast up accounts into my bunk."

"Do you know, I feel as if you and I might have been friends since—oh, long ago. Sherry wrote to me so often, *Fleming has*, and *Fleming says*, that now you are come to Bournebrook it seems I know you already."

He gave a little bow and a half-quirk of his smile. "I am most honored you should say so, but terrified, madam, to think Sherry might have had my measure complete. Surely there is something of me you do not know."

"Surely. Do you speak so much or so well on any subject but horses, for a start?"

"Ah, no. Not in company." He made one of his queer horse-

49

fashion tilts of the head and reached his left hand out, half toward her, as if to push aside the sudden silence. Harriet neglected to step away. "It is late—and grown cold. May I see you to the house?"

"There is no need," said Harriet, when he did not touch her. "It is perhaps best you did not. I cannot say whether Cousin Beauchamp is abed, and her tongue will grind though we give it no grist."

The captain reached his frock coat from a nail by Malabar's door and settled it round Harriet. It was redolent of straw and stable, having hung since morning among the barn frocks; he winced, though Harriet did not. "Beg pardon, I ought to have thought of—I have no other."

"I would not have you freezing for my heedlessness," Harriet protested, and took up the well-broken lapels to return it.

With both hands, fast and firmly, Fleming did the buttons up to her throat. "Only leave it where I might find it before morning."

Harriet nodded. A layer of black wool, glossed with wear and brushing, and a dozen indifferent pewter buttons; Sherry might have cast it in the rag-bag, and of a sudden she did not want to give it up. She had never had a thought so foolish.

"Thank you," she said, when she remembered her manners.

His hands had scarce left her. She could think of nothing else to say.

"Your servant, madam."

"Goodnight, Captain." She meant full well to speak more to him—something, anything—but he had stepped back into his horse's box, singing softly, fragments of *Mary Ambrey*.

CHAPTER 6

"You spy," she hissed. "You contemptible sneak, you—" Harriet broke off, backing the captain half against the library table and cramming the manuscript into her pocket, though pages twisted and rent. "I'll kill you. I'll kill you with a table knife. You *stoat*."

"For reading, madam, in a library?"

"We had no one stirring through old broadsheets before you came." There was still a trace of murder in her expression. She re-stacked and flattened the mildewed papers, shoving them into a corner so that her own eyes watered, but the captain did not give her the satisfaction of a sneeze. "Sherry comes here not at all—and it is no matter to conceal a little new amongst so many old."

"You are Mr. Darracott? *Red Lady of Hardwick Hall*, Cyprian Darracott?"

She neither blushed nor blanched, though Fleming did.

"Hellfire, where d'you get such lurid stuff?"

"Revenge plays," shrugged Harriet. "History books. It was all such a ruin," she went on. "I know one doesn't speak of such things, of finances, but Sherry was out on the Peninsula and the estate was in dreadful disorder… and now he is home, and I may as well keep him comfortably."

"Your cousin—she must know? Is that why she's such an antidote toward you?"

"Oh, no! Dorcas hates me because she is a walking, speaking gooseberry fool, and I was young enough once to tell her so. If she knew of Mr. Darracott, she'd blackmail me blind."

"Best stow that, then," said Fleming. He shifted to stand between Harriet and the library's open door. "It's only she wears such heels on her half-boots."

Harriet spared enough silence to listen out into the corridor. In half a minute her cousin would pass into sight, and they into hers.

"You read all of it?"

"Yes, all of it." He barely braced when she shoved him. "Meantime I had rather hide, madam, unless you see another way from here!"

"There are ways all over this house," answered Harriet.

"Sherry knows them best, but…" She considered the open door and the quick-clicking heels in the passage, and took the captain's wrist. With his weight and hers she pressed at a worn-down bit of scrollwork along a bookcase. He found stairs, by tripping up along them; then the bookcase swung, silent, to nip at his heels, and in the dark Harriet was tugging him higher.

They came up short against the frame of an old window, all that remained, Fleming thought, of a turret room now enclosed. When he would have leant against the glass and regained a breath, Harriet scarcely paused. She opened the window, caught up her skirts, and ducked out.

The wind howled. The half-clouded afternoon was bright as rocketry after the depth-dark stair, and Fleming balked. "The roof?"

She stepped from the oak sill out onto the leads. "Indeed, unless you prefer the library, and my cousin."

"Why is it—how is it, madam, you come over hare-brained when I must follow?"

"*Must*," scoffed Harriet, and Fleming knew he had erred, height or no height to dizzy him. She stood against the embrasure nearest, though the stone was tilting and time-bitten, and did not flinch at the drop.

"Harry, mind the edge."

"Upon my word, I mind it." She would not regard him, but

gestured out to the hills bordered dark by the sea. "This is the edge of the world, to me."

"Would you go further, if you could?"

"By God, yes! I wish I'd been born a man. I might have taken ship and fought for England, and have at least a medal to show for my life."

"Or nothing to show for it." He said it reasonably, and weary.

"I'd have learned things of use, then, before dying. How to climb a rigging. How to shoot."

"Carabine or pistol?"

"Oh, you mean to teach me!"

"If you wish."

"It's not so simple! If I woke tomorrow a shot like Sherry— if I learnt your manage for horses in the night—still I'd be female."

He gazed out to the horizon, and after a moment let go his death-grip on the embrasure to take her hand.

"You write adventures well enough, female or no."

"That's for Sherry. For the tenants, for bread on the table. And it's all rubbish, it's not—you cannot understand," fumbled Harriet, before the wind could snatch the words away. "What it is to be scorned for weakness, to be left behind—to be made invisible!"

She was not invisible now. Captain Fleming had shed his seven-league stare and looked for all the world as if he did understand; with his thumbs he brushed back the tears from Harriet's cheeks.

A moment's fumbling, lips against teeth, chill noses all out of place, and Captain Fleming's fingers went loose in her hair. Harriet slid her own hand into his queued curls, rested her cheek against his and would not let him shrug away. With the second kiss he recalled the art, how two people fit and breathed together; and then he pulled back, his look when he met her eyes half daring, half stunned.

"Nathaniel." She spoke and felt him shiver. "Again. Please."

"That is my chair, Spaniel."

"An excellent chair," the captain agreed. He did not hurry out of it, nor move at all.

"That's never my gl—"

"An excellent brandy, if you must drink your wine as sugar."

"How much of it's got down you, man?"

Captain Fleming appeared to calculate. In truth he was not

much out of order; every hair of his queue lay in place. When he spoke, "Oh, one or five," he was once more quiet, steady, just a touch mocking of the Major or himself. He stood, unwavering, and offered the lame man's chair.

"And what on earth's kept you waking?"

"Same as you, I m'n wager." But Fleming looked to the chimneypiece clock and his eyebrows rose. "I came in to ask you the loan of your racing saddle. I fear the time escaped me."

The last made Sherbourne bear the candle close to him. "Spaniel, you've come over peculiar. Have another with me, and find your bunk."

Standing, he had gone restive; he angled himself toward the chamber door, gripped his elbows behind his back and could not still his feet. The captain did not refuse half a glass of spirits.

"Now I know you've gone off it," said Sherbourne. "You've not taken a drop since you puked up my good stuff at Orthez."

"Bloody hackbones drove the ball in deeper. You cast your share up when he set that leg!"

If both shivered, the wind off the water had risen to drive at Sherbourne's windows. He filled his own glass again, and sank in his chair with the rough-set leg out before him. "Never mind what's in your head, then, if you don't see fit to tell me; but you can't want that saddle now, it's gone eleven."

"I'd find now sufficient," disagreed Fleming.

"And what for? Have you stolen a hot-blood from the Gypsies and hid him in my stables?"

Now, faintly, girlishly, he blushed. "I thought to ask for your Barbary roan, as well, sir. Only—only so far as the park."

"My racing saddle, my hot-blood roan, and my park! You'll ask for my sister next, and the tack to suit her!"

"Mmnf," said Fleming, and his color in candlelight went extraordinary.

"Take the horse," Sherbourne answered him. "In daylight. No man's gotten a headstall on Harry, never mind riding— oh, be excused, Captain, before you choke on your own spittle!"

He shouted, and half got up from the chair, before the captain could flee. "That's it, I'd wager the bloody Barbary's four legs! Come back, you scoundrel, and let me see your face!"

"Major?"

"Must have my racing saddle, indeed! It's a *woman* troubles him, Captain Fleming has found a woman! An Englishwoman, and from Bournesea village!"

"Hush, Sherry, for God's sake." A moan of misery escaped him; the captain hid in his hands.

"It's above your rank to hush me, you bonny bastard. I can't account you've gone mad for a woman since I stole the last one from you. Who on earth is she?"

"You did not steal Sabine!"

"There is a supper ball in three days' time," went on Sherbourne, though Fleming had not uncovered his face. "I gave no thought to it—Lord! Harry hates 'em—but every young woman for twenty miles will be there; surely yours will be."

"I could not say," answered Fleming.

"You might *smile* about her without foiling etiquette. Look here, are you so cross I've found you out?"

"ARSE DOWN ON YOUR HEEL," Sherbourne bellowed, not yet come fully past the box hedge. "It's a gun, you're not proposing ma—*Harry!*"

The rifle's stock lay steady, and Harriet did not hang fire.

"My *Whitney*," he added. "How came you by it?"

She gazed back at him, over her shoulder, silent.

"As if anyone in this house heeds *me*."

"It is a lovely gun, the captain gives me to understand," Harriet said. Then she turned away from him, lowering her crouch as Sherbourne had directed. "He said it would be best."

"Best what?" He had had time to take her measure, in boots —Captain Fleming's boots, he thought—and breeches the worse for her kneeling on the grass, but a longer string of words he could not manage.

"…Teaching," Harriet replied, sighted down the barrel, and fired. At the flash and recoil Sherbourne flinched harder than she did. He saw her exhale hard, but there seemed no surprise or pain in it.

"And where is the captain?"

"Gone for more powder."

"The better I may stuff it down his shirt and light it, leaving a woman alone with a gun!"

"I asked the captain to show me."

"Arse," said Sherbourne, as he had said it once already. "Why not ask me?"

"You'd have refused me." Harriet stood and pantomimed reloading, with a twist of paper cast onto the lawn and a bit of shot held in her teeth, and scoured the charge home before Sherbourne realized she was not pretending, at all.

He put his hand out for the rifle, and Harriet did not cede it. "Sister, I'll give it back."

"It's my last charge," she protested.

"It's my bloody gun!" He lowered his voice, and did not look at her, standing as she did with grains of powder sparkling on her cheek. "Where is your target?"

"The elm—fifty yards out."

If he shaded his eyes he could see it, a span of butcher's paper with a broad outline in ink. The left side of the paper was blown full of holes.

"A pretty thing for you to be doing when I've paid twenty pounds for a supper-ball tonight. Haven't you punch-cups to arrange? Village halls to festoon? Here." Sherbourne pulled his handkerchief from his sleeve. "Take this out, if you please, and spare me the walk. Ninety paces past your elm."

"Eighty yards," Harriet calculated, and frowned at him. "Sherry—"

"D'you doubt a man of my age might make the shot?"

"I don't doubt you, brother." She started away, a little uncertain in the boots, and returned across the lawn to look openmouthed at Sherbourne.

He was gazing at her as if he had gone soft-witted, and he held the Whitney rifle out to her by the forestock.

"Sherry?"

"Present arms, then."

Harriet obeyed, slowly, looking at him sidewise all the while.

"Bring on," said Sherbourne, "and lock." He moved behind her, without touching her or lending advice.

"Waste of a ball," Harriet muttered. "This distance. You wish to be proven right, you wish I might look a fool—"

He laid his hand between her shoulder blades, then, and spoke low by her ear. "I don't doubt you."

"I HAVE NOT SEEN the captain, Cousin. Do you suppose he means to appear?"

"He is an officer; he will be in time." Harriet plucked at her sash, though it could not lie more smoothly, and dampened her fingers in a vase of gaudy nerines, to school her curls.

"And do you suppose he owns dancing shoes, Harriet dear? They are rather costly. But our Sherry vouches for him as an excellent dancer. Smelling of horse!"

She was in too good humor to rise to it. She went on, half dreamily, without a thought for her cousin's ears. "Ambergris, rather, and...himself."

Dorcas snorted. "How you should know that, I have no wish to calculate. Dear Aunt Caro—"

"Is not here." Not even thoughts of the dowager countess Sherbourne could make her flinch. "And what does she care for me? She has not forgiven any of us the loss of her figure. I much doubt she would notice if Captain Fleming danced, or licked Sherry's ear, or fell into the punch."

"Harriet Georgiana, you are carrying on with this man to vex me!"

"Why, Dorcas! Did you want him?"

If Harriet had been a hand's breadth closer, her cousin might have slapped her on the cheek. "Have you utterly forgotten who you are?"

"Indeed, that is one of the nicest things about him, that for a moment I might breathe and be myself." Harriet gave a full, sweet smile. "Is it not just so with you and Beauchamp?"

Dorcas looked as if hot ash filled her shoes. In her silence, Harriet stole away into the garden; she would pay for it later, in gossip spread or trinkets ruined, but for now she cared only for getting clean away. It was a warm night and clear, just passing eight o'clock; in Bournesea village the linkmen were beginning to light the lamps. There was candle-gleam at Sherbourne's window, where to the last minute he would change one cravat-knot for another, spill scent bottles, dismiss footmen—any thing to avoid stepping foot in the landau; Captain Fleming's room lay dark.

He leant against the hayfield's boundary oak, somewhat twisted so braid and bark would not snag together. His dancing shoes had once been very fine; made for him— without boots, he had feet uncommon small—and all pale silk, with starry clocks picked out in blue, so that they matched the Seventh's regimentals.

"I despaired," Nathaniel whispered, and then he took her hand. "They have seen to the harnesses half an hour since."

"Do you mind so very much, then, being late?" Harriet drew close enough, in the shadows, to touch the captain's collar and trace her fingers against his cheek.

"Madam, I have no chronometer to speak of." For half a minute Captain Fleming stood scarcely breathing, content to rest his gloved hand on her arm, perhaps, her shoulder; then Harriet made some small sound, and the gap between them closed. He kissed her like a man home from the war.

"It is curious," remarked Harriet. "Sherry used always to dance, on home leave. I cannot think his leg pains him enough to keep him from it now."

Captain Fleming studied his cup of punch, looking neither

to Harriet nor Sherbourne, who was across the room from the musicians and looked to have swallowed a storm cloud.

"Were you there, sir, when he was injured?"

"Quite so," said Fleming, at last. He might have been waiting for a dip in the music. "His Kestrel—his horse, madam—was killed under him at Genappe. He could not get clear in time."

"How appalling," said Harriet. "When he wrote from Brussels, he said only that his leg was broken. He might have had an accident in the street!"

The captain studied a threadbare patch on his dancing shoe. Fleming had sent that letter, over Sherbourne's faltering mark; it had not told one tithe the truth. "It is a soldier's habit, I am afraid, to make little of what those at home might deem great; certainly Sherry never expected to make old bones."

"Do you think he suffers the nostalgia? One reads that some men caught it, in the war."

"No, madam, and I do not think it catching, like the measles. I think it lives in the souls of fighting men, and memory brings it out."

Harriet's satin-gloved hand brushed the sleeve of Fleming's coat and was gone, before anyone might remark.

"Will you not dance, lady?"

"Yes, in half a moment," answered Harriet, "but I like to hear you talk of my brother." She went on, half to herself, "he is much changed."

The musicians had struck up a sauteuse, nearly all at once and in time; the din and whirl and the clap of dancing-shoes on the boards grew so much greater that Fleming had to lean down to her, when she spoke again.

"…something, Captain, in your confidence?"

"Upon my honor, madam."

"Did my brother have a woman at Paris?"

Fleming did not spray his punch upon the room. He passed his hand over his eyes a moment, and set the little cup carefully aside. "I rather think we should dance."

"But I am forever turning my ankles at this one. Might you induce Sherry to do so? It is a gentleman's duty to look to the wallflowers."

"Madam, I fear I am not fetching in slippers and a skirt."

Harriet laughed. "Then I will leave him to his devices for tonight, but Captain, I do not excuse you from my question."

"I will trade an answer for the slow waltz," said Fleming solemnly.

"Surely, and the quadrille, and *Roger de Coverley*, if you are not promised."

"Unless you would rather I dance with Sherry…?"

As it was Michaelmas, they were obliged to wait through *John Barleycorn*; the captain offered for Harriet's arm, but she stayed seated. "I shan't waste the set on a song I mislike," said Harriet. "And do you wait and see if anyone else offers it me!"

No one did. There were not so many genteel families between Thaxted and the sea as to provide dancing-partners for spinsters, Fleming supposed, though there was not a lovelier woman in the room.

"Were it Sherry's own ball, of course, someone would fall on his sword, but here they have all grown used to my waiting. The young men all want young wives, and the married men all want…"

"A night with your cousin?"

Harriet laughed. Her gown was white as any girl's, but her sash and bandeau were of an evening-primrose silk that Viscountess Beauchamp had brought from Town; Fleming had witnessed the disorder, that afternoon, when the new colour made the Viscountess look like a waxwork whose liver was poorly. Now she tripped through the set in the scarlet trimmings bullied from Harriet, all trace of vexation subdued with talcum heavily applied, and beguiled four men to whom she was not wed.

"John Barleycorn must die," Harriet murmured. "It is as well. There is Sergeant Cooper with her, of the Ninety-Fifth; she has two children already by the Rifles. That is quite like fidelity, with Dorcas."

"Madam, your waltz," said Fleming, and bowed, and looked much relieved that the music excused his saying more.

"Charmed, Captain."

"Outside…or center?"

"Oh, Captain, why should we not take the center? It will entertain Bournesea village for simply weeks."

"We were three years at Paris to keep the peace," said Fleming, as they turned in careful orbits round the floor. "Sherry much felt the loss of his men. Indeed he may have…dallied."

"I believe it must have been more than that. Beauchamp said, this morning, that the women of France were all…"

"Whores," suggested Fleming.

"You need not blush, sir. I have heard my brother use the very word in company. But Sherry looked ready to call Beauchamp out. He da'sn't—Beauchamp is swimming in the ready, and God knows we are not; he would only bring suit, if Sherry tried it."

"I should quite like to see a suit brought by a dead man." Fleming smiled. It was not a friendly one.

"Oh! Beauchamp would simply make the Recording Angel his man of business. But the whole affair—it made me think, sir. Something must have happened to stir Sherbourne's feeling."

"There was a woman," said Fleming, keeping note of Harriet's countenance. He was exceeding careful with his next words. "I believe Sherbourne would have made her his wife. I dare say I believe they should have been happy."

"Why did he not marry her?"

"She had been—ah—one of the prime articles of the Imperial Guard, before we gave them the rout."

"If Sherry gave two figs for that, I should love him the less!"

"Upon my word, he pressed his case with her. She said she would not let him shame himself at home. He was the Earl by then, madam."

"The more reason he should have married her, if Father were not alive to preach at him!"

"That is not mine to say, madam, but he cannot now marry her. She is dead."

CHAPTER 7

The night air and the dancing ought to have
driven her to sleep with the rest of Sherbourne's
household, but *The Mysteries of Udolpho*, and mares' heads
lowering over the cliffs, had acted the opposite. Thoughts of
Captain Fleming in the part of Valancourt did not quite
balance with brigands in the clothes-press and silver daggers
in every flash of lightning. Harriet passed perhaps half an
hour past two o'clock clutching her bed-hangings shut; then
she gave it up, called herself an idiot blithering whining
flinching girl, took a candle and a shawl and quit the room.

The rain was loud enough to keep every sound from her,
save for a moment's sharp snore when she passed
Sherbourne's rooms, but when the slap of water and the
wind off the sea subsided a moment, Harriet heard
something below. Not brigands, surely— if someone had
come to rob Bournebrook in dead of night, they would have

brought a lantern, and Harriet wanted more than her small light to make her way to the first floor. The drawing-room door was open, but only the last of the firelight, lighter gray in the rain-muffled dark, showed out to where Harriet stood. She went up to the threshold and no one hailed her, dead or living; no one within was rifling the whatnots or knocking over urns. She was about to close the door and count herself a fool again when someone sobbed, very low.

"What on earth!"

Fleming sat in the window-seat, turned so that he must face the storm. His knees were pulled to his chest, his arms were locked round his knees, and his face was hidden. In his plain shirt and buff breeches and stockings, he gleamed white as any ghost by Harriet's candle.

"Nathaniel?"

He did not lift his head. Close to, she saw his arms and back all trembling, and when Harriet touched his shoulder he cried out.

"Captain!"

Fleming had been weeping, as Harriet had not known men wept, and his voice was raw with tears. "Please, I pray—I beg you leave me."

Harriet went only far enough to light half a dozen candles, and tip half a day's coal over the fender to liven the fire. "I shall, if you like, now that you do not freeze in the dark."

"What care I for that, when my men are all out in the rain?" He did not adorn it with politeness. His voice soared up and cracked. She might have gone, then, but in the next lightning-flash, she saw his eyes.

"You ought not sit up alone." Harriet climbed into the window-seat, decent far from him; she tucked her nightclothes round her feet, and cast her shawl over Fleming. The captain flinched. His shoulders rose, his back rounded, and then, as he could not get further away, he fell still.

Harriet had not thought to light a marked candle. It seemed an hour they sat in vigil, not quite touching, never speaking. The rain rattled like shot at the windows, and the thunder could not seem to spend itself. Fleming stared through the dark without respite.

The first of the candles had guttered, and the fire was giving way at the window to creeping cold, when she dared address him again.

"Will you look at me, Nathaniel, and not the dead?"

He unfolded, at last, and faced her; his hand closed upon hers and he drew breath almost calmly, as if he would speak. But no words came aloud, and the only word Harriet knew for his countenance was *pain*. It showed on him like blood from a wound.

"Hush," said Harriet, put her arms round his neck, and kissed him.

THE VILLAGE BELOW was snarled with French dragoons, and Major Hodge's squadron had gone forward and not returned. Now the Seventh was all called to saddle, straining for sight down a narrow farm lane banked with hills, down toward a foe they could not see. Arrayed for the charge, columns tight, the men waited and watched the smoke rise from below.

"Orders, Major?" Eleanor had given her company leave to drop pelisses, in this swelter; she could hear them chafing and muttering behind her, and Malabar's head was low. In an hour it might rain, but for now it was three o' the clock in the middle of June, and the dust of the road made the men squint and cough.

Sherbourne squinted down the road through the defile. "My lord Uxbridge has honored us with the charge, so I suppose we must not refuse it. I will not wait upon Hodge any longer. Fraser, harry them 'pon the right, and Gordon, Peters, do you take the left."

The din of Fraser's bugler sounded limp in the steaming air. Eleanor put a hand up to shield her ear, and flick her queue off her neck.

"Fleming," came Sherbourne's call. "Be my eyes; take 'em front. I shan't loiter!"

She nodded, and signaled her company from the column. They were better-drilled than some, but it took time for them to absorb the signal, to close canteens and check sabre-grips. Sherbourne came close by her mount while she waited and reached out, not to offer a touch for luck but to grip her elbow, hard.

"'Thaniel," he said, very low. "It is as likely Hodge is dead, and his squadron with him."

"I know, Major."

"It don't sit well with me, sending the men down the neck of a bottle to —" Sherbourne was compelled to pause, as of a sudden the dust made his voice thick. "If the wind blows ill, look after my sister."

"Aye, Major!" She said aloud, as she might answer any command, for the major's comfort and the men's. She drew her sabre and tapped Sherbourne's hilts, then held the steel aloft to catch the sun. Behind her the company was still, waiting for her sabre's forward fall.

"The Seventh will advance!" Sherbourne stood to full height in the saddle and bellowed the order. "Oh, and Fleming! Break them."

"Company, advance!" She shouted at her lungs' reach, with courage all unfelt. Sherbourne shouted something after her, about an errand, but Eleanor had passed too far ahead to make any reply. Her left hand went into Malabar's mane, and she was grateful beyond all things that no one could see her face. She had not the first idea what to do. Break a line of cuirassiers, she supposed, with ninety men!

There was little time enough for thinking. Her light-stepping grey was the sharp point of an arrow flying fast; just behind, her young lieutenants whipped the dust up in the road. Round a curve she could *suddenly see the French troops arraying, not cuirassiers but lancers— bloody lancers!*

The air was rent with whistling, sour with smoke. A shower of rockets —English rockets, God bless Sherbourne, that had been his errand— sprayed with pops and shrieks upon the lancers' line.

"Lovely weather, is it not!" Sherbourne was laughing, as he came along her company's column, his white Kestrel swift as any bullet; the rest of the squadron held to his wake, and Fleming was not alone. "I told you I'd not loiter!"

She gave him a nod.

"Don't be cross, 'Thaniel! Give Fraser's lads a moment to work, and we'll take 'em at the jump!" Kestrel thundered into step with Malabar, and Sherbourne was near enough for her to take his measure. He was iron sober, his grin gone fierce; he meant indeed to face the lancers at the jump.

The uhlans blocked the road ahead, peppered as they were with falling flame; the ground, the seconds, Eleanor's breath fell away as she realized it was all going to go wrong. The enemy line was like iron, lances down and fixed. No Englishmen stung them upon the left or right.

"Fraser, where is Fraser," she called across to Sherbourne.

"Almighty God," Eleanor heard him say, and then—

Someone's hand was tight across her mouth. Eleanor struggled and struck out.

"Captain!" Harriet was close by her, rough-whispered as though she had started out of sleep. "Oh, hush!"

Fleming stared up at her, bleary, heart thudding away like hooves.

"You shouted," Harriet explained. "I'm sorry—I did not intend—it is morning," she finished, her countenance all dread. "I feared…"

"Did I strike you?"

"You missed," shrugged Harriet. The drawing-room was cold, dark except for the white-edged gray of dawn at the windows. When Fleming moved, he tumbled from the window-seat with a thump.

"Someone is above." He thrust Harriet's shawl up toward her, sparing a hand to rub his head where it had met the floor. "Stay here, and if anyone questions, you may say you nodded off reading."

"What on earth will you do?"

"Flee by the window, madam."

She could not help smiling at him when he smiled so. "Give you good morning, Nathaniel," Harriet whispered, as he pulled on his boots and climbed again to the window-seat.

"Servant, Harry."

CHAPTER 8

*F*leming found her in the long gallery, when she did not come to breakfast, and approached softly in hope that it would seem he did not seek her at all. When he knew the game was up he slouched his weight in his boots, making them echo upon the parquet, and made a show of whistling *Lilibullero.* He had kept pace to a drum for a good many years; it helped him keep a measured step now, when he saw she had been crying.

"Good morning, madam."

"Good morning," Harriet answered, blotting her cheek with her shawl. "Pray excuse my countenance, Captain. I have only been in discourse with Cousin Beauchamp again."

Fleming drew back. "Is she about? Would you have me ring for a chaperone?"

"She never comes here." Harriet sounded weary. Her shawl of undyed wool, her hair still caught up in a cap, and—somehow—the proud set of her shoulders made her seem diminished. Fleming thought of keeping his peace.

"If we were men, I should call her out! It is damned unfair." Harriet stood up straighter, propped by anger; she seemed to return to herself again. "But you have come round out of the way to speak to me, Captain."

"I meant only to say, madam, that I must leave for London upon the midday mail."

"Leave Bournebrook! So soon! Does Sherry know you mean to leave us?"

"I have mentioned it to him, madam, and I hope conveyed my thanks."

"We—Sherry will miss you terribly." Harriet paused, and her eyes narrowed. "Please, tell me no one dressed as a gentlewoman has accused you of riding Sherry's coat-sleeves, or—"

"No! I wish it were so easily ignored. Matter of a roof; of weather, rather. My sister has given me the freedom of her house in Town, and I must have it looked over. It has not been repaired or refitted since Napoleon left Elba; I have had notice it's half under water, and likely even the mice have given it quits."

"Then you will be in Town Christmastide, and New Year's,"

said Harriet. "You must stop with us a while at Sherry's house. Cousin Beauchamp's musicales never have ballads! You will write to m—my brother, in the meantime?"

"As often as I may, madam, and Sherbourne has my direction."

Harriet smiled at him, briefly. The long gallery, its narrow windows crowded about with portraiture, was very chill; at the far end of the room were the doors to the shut-up west wing, and draught and darkness seemed to creep round their edges. Fleming offered for Harriet's arm, and she took his in a tight clasp. Under her ancestors' watch, Harriet shivered.

"I hope there is not a ghost at Bournebrook, madam?"

"There ought to be many." Harriet said. "The Earls have given much for king and country, but the second sons have always been wreckers. My grandsire was said to have been a most lawless man."

She looked back over her shoulder as if that gentleman stood waiting. "There are tunnels under this house straight through Bournesea village and to the cliffs, for the men to bring the spoils in."

Fleming hardly realized they had been walking as she spoke, back to the inhabited parts of the house; the portraits were newer and brighter, and close by the gallery doors there was a triptych, untouched by dust, though draped in dusty black.

"My sisters," Harriet said, pausing as though she introduced them at a ball. "Helena, Hestia, and Honoria. When I felt disagreeable, I sounded the *H*."

Each had sat for the painter, perhaps, upon her engagement; each was gowned and sashed in silvered white. They were three near copies of Harriet and Sherbourne, all fair as milk with dark, wild-curling hair, not quite smoothed down even in the paintings.

"It is why I will not marry, Captain, and Sherry will not press me."

"Beg pardon?"

"My sisters were all very happily married. They left me in mortal dread of it."

"What on earth, Harry," replied Fleming. "Sherbourne would meet any man who mistreated you, surely."

"Childbirth, Captain," Harriet got out, and waited for Fleming to stammer or blush. "I have no wish to ever get a child. All three of my sisters were brought to bed and died. We have one nephew to show for it."

"I am heartily grieved for it, madam." The captain inclined his head. "But—Harry—if your cousins should press upon Sherry, and so press you, and you wished a respite…"

Harriet looked baffled. Fleming had to look at the ceiling.

"…you would come to no danger if you married me."

"What on earth!"

"I cannot give you children, Harry, even should you wish it."

"Oh. Oh, Nathaniel, I am sorry."

A BACHELOR MAY NOT properly correspond with an unmarried lady. It was her grandmother's advice, to a girl from another lifetime. Fleming rubbed the ink-bottle in her hands to warm it.

My dear lady,

My very dear Harriet—

Harry, Eleanor wrote at last. She was near nodding over the page, much though she wished to write. Her fingernails, where she could note them by the rushlight, were blackened and broken, and her hand was cramping round the quill.

My sister's house in Mayfair I found a ruin, and I have had much work to bring it up to mark. This should not concern me if I did not miss your society so very much. As it is I fear I cannot extend Sherbourne the supper invitation I meant, as the kitchens have lately lain under four inches of water, and I have not found a cook willing to swim. How fares Phantom of Fotheringhay? I never knew history so blood curdling.

She filled a sheet and a half, leaving a back blank for folding, conversing upon trivialities as though Harriet was with her in the room. Her study was small, made chill by the windows giving light from the street below, and it was furnished with the flotsam of years; it cheered Eleanor a great deal to think of Harriet here, even if she could not imagine her so far upstairs, taking her ease in a chair whose seat might drop at any moment.

Next morning, having paid to advertise for a charwoman on Saturdays, and done herself the extravagance of a pound of candles, Eleanor posted the letter. She was scarcely home again, eating a pork-pie wrapped in a handkerchief to keep it from the dirt of her hands, when a post-boy knocked at the knockerless door. There was a letter from Bournesea, Essex, but not from Sherbourne.

Not until Eleanor read the first lines, standing against the staircase, did she realize she had given the boy a half-devoured pork-pie with his fee.

Dear Nathaniel,

Sherbourne having travelled to visit our Mother, I pled Cold in the Head, took the liberty of going over his Study, and discovered your Direction. Pray forgive me being so forward as to write so soon.

Harriet wrote a small, plain hand, with no flourishes, and the letter ran three sheets.

It was never more than a handful of days, after that, before a letter arrived. Eleanor kept them tucked into the slats of the box-bed in the chamber she had taken for herself. As

October raced toward Guy Fawkes' Night, that did not suffice; the earliest ones she bound up and stowed in her campaign chest, hidden safe among her mother's things. Until she found a small hoard of coin in her grandmother's Sunday-box, Eleanor's diet tended sharpish toward brown bread and postage.

At last, a week past Martinmas, word came from Sherbourne that he and his sister would return to Town in a fortnight. Eleanor left off sorting the silver, weeding what could be scoured from what could be sold, in the middle of the day; she had had, for a time, some words in mind to send.

Harry, she got down, scarce able to credit her daring. The quill-slip did not quite fit, or else Eleanor's hand shook, and the next line jogged down the page.

My prospects are narrower, and my graces fewer, than you deserve, but I would ask leave to court you.

She put her mark to it formal and with flourish, *Capt Nathaniel Jas Fleming 7ᵗʰ Her Majesty the Queen's*, and let it go into the mail-boy's hand with a shilling for speed.

The reply was a half-sheet folded over, sealed with an unfamiliar wafer, and it arrived by evening the next day. There was no date, no mark from Harriet, and no greeting.

Yes.

CHAPTER 9

*H*arriet was late coming down to the salon. No one gave account to spinsters when the room was packed with girls in their first season—was not her brother the Earl yet a bachelor? All the huntresses looked one to Harriet, each too young for Sherbourne, and above half too vapid; were they taught at all to converse any more, these blossoms of English girlhood? Her own sisters had been known upon the Marriage Mart as much for wit as fine ankles, and that was not so very long ago…

One of the candyfloss maidens trod Harriet's foot, and made no remark of it as she nudged past into the salon.

"Very bad *ton*, you know, dovey," said Harriet in clenched teeth, more cross at herself for woolgathering than for the mark upon her new dancing shoe.

"Are you quite well, Lady Harry?"

"Dear Linton, if such occurrences troubled me, I should never emerge from my cloud of blue devils," she smiled, a little false. "Will you inquire for me whether Captain Fleming is arrived?"

"He waited you, my lady, but now he is within, as some of the company asked for music; the hired players are not yet come." Linton paused. "If I may, Lady Harry, that new green gives your form every credit."

"Heavens," said Harriet, blushing unaccountably. Her brother's man was one of few in the house quite old enough to marry Sherbourne.

"Shall I announce you, madam?"

"Oh, don't, pray. I cannot abide a scene tonight." Her head throbbed at the prospect of the night before her, of another season. The captain's letter had given her joy, of a kind, but not hope. She had not seen him these three months, and she might gain the salon to find his every dance taken by a woman younger.

"Lady Harry?" Linton stood aside the door. "Will you not go in?"

She could not have moved, just then, had Linton shoved her. At the far corner of the room, where the harp and pianoforte had been shifted for the evening's use, she spied her brother's dark head bent beside Fleming's fair one. Their music was some of Sherry's beloved Schubert—she thought the *Serenade*—and they went along in such rhythm, Harriet scarcely knew which man played what part.

"I did not know he could play so," said Linton, who knew whether Sherbourne dressed to the left or right. Harriet touched his arm a moment, and then stepped over the threshold. She had for cover the room's applause for the Earl, and the sight of the captain in his regimentals lent resolve to her step. He had left off his pelisse, for playing, and his shoulders were as fine as Harriet remembered. He was conversing with Sherry, aside, as Harriet came near, and something Sherry said made Fleming's countenance all mirth.

"You will suffer, if you insist," Fleming gave Sherbourne answer. "I don't sing to myself, you know. I'm not in voice."

"For her, then," said Sherbourne, and goosed at the captain's ribs.

She was caught quite out.

"My lady Harriet," Fleming greeted her, stood, and gave his deepest bow.

"S-sir. I hope you are well."

"*Sir*," echoed Sherbourne. "Great God, man, you might have mentioned."

"Mentioned what, Major?"

"Nothing at all," said Sherbourne, jumping up from the

pianoforte's bench with briskness strange to see in a lamed man. "Leave you then, shall I? All manner of people to see, say nothing of keeping Beauchamp from my brandy."

Fleming looked after him in something like dismay. "Think you he disapproves of us? I thought—with your cousin so in his ear—he must know."

"I know Cousin Beauchamp told him—at Bournebrook— she made it out to him that we…" Harriet swallowed. "He had no harsh words for me on the matter, but you were gone from us, by then. I think we must stake his good nature upon the Christmas-punch."

"She made out to him, that we *what?*"

A footman came, then, as Fleming had not returned to his seat at the pianoforte; the liveryman handed the captain's sabre. It was a dress sword, plated over with gilt and silver; a motto ran down from the hilts.

"May I?" Harriet asked, and took the sabre without waiting the captain's assent. Cousin Beauchamp was not in sight, in any case, for Fleming to skewer her upon it; Harriet had time to collect the motto, and read, roughly, *"Acies ad Hostem."*

"It means—"

"Sharp edge toward enemy," Harriet finished.

"It was my gift from Sherbourne, when I rose captain," Fleming said. "He thought I should need the advice."

"Has your carcass blighted my settee since last night?" Sherbourne was half-dressed, though it rose one o'clock; he nudged at Fleming with the brass head of his walking-stick.

"Ah, Major! Cold gotten into your leg, then? Filled you with goodwill toward men?"

"Stow your insufferable cheer," Sherbourne groaned. "I suppose you must be in good humor, Golden-Locks?"

"Indeed, I am. I was thinking of Moorlowe at Christmastide." The captain reached across from where he sprawled upon the sofa, rounding up cloves from a saucer on the tea-table and studding them into an orange. He did not sit up, only regarding Sherbourne over the turned-out toes of his shoes. "Dare say you would call it no more than a hunting box, but I love it."

"Have you seen it, inside ten years?"

"No," said Fleming. "But it is my home."

"Happen tha r'turn to Yorkshire…" began Sherbourne, more broadly than was kind. Fleming sat up just enough to hurl the clove-orange into Sherbourne's trouser front.

"Ow! Bastard! If you were to return home, I suppose you mean to go leg-shackled to my sister?"

"I beg your pardon?" Fleming flailed and scrabbled and came upright.

"It seemed to me, last night, that you and she had perhaps —ah—she was most pleased to see you."

"I was most gratified that she should join us. I was much in her society at Bournebrook, and I dare say she converses rather well."

"Spaniel, you kissed her!"

"I?" The captain gazed up, surpassing unruffled.

"Kissed her hand, at least, in my sight, and—"

"She is a lady gently bred, and I dare say a friend!"

"Friend, nothing! Think you I have abstained long enough to mistake a woman thoroughly kissed?"

"Your house is shored up at the beams by kissing-boughs! It might have been a dozen beaux with nothing to do, as every girl in the party was launched at your head."

"Might," Sherbourne bit out.

"I wish you would not abstain, Sherry, or else make it known—"

"Let us keep to the subject, Spaniel, of your making free with my sister!"

"Upon my word, I have not meant to make free with her. Too long at Paris, I guess, where it is no *on dit* if one touches a lady's glove. And she is witty, Sherry, and most kind."

"*Harry* is?" Sherbourne snorted. "*Mignon*, when she had her season, she left seven men in gory pools of their own pride. Scoffed at posy-rings from Bath to John o'Groats. Never I heard the poor beggars deem her *kind*."

"Haven't blunt enough for a posy-ring, so it's as well." Fleming shrugged.

"She's too old for such things!"

"She is two years the younger, scoundrel, am I in my dotage?"

"…How on earth should you know that?"

Fleming neglected to make a sound.

"Look here, I don't care if you dally with my sister; I'd be touched in the upper workings if I thought I might prevent her. Only this is Town, not backwater Bournesea…"

"I shall consider myself advised, Major."

"Oh. Well. It is only—I rather thought—come in to luncheon, Spaniel, never mind it. Roasted a pig, you know. Christmas."

"Sure you want to go in there, Fleming? It's a rout." Linton had taken a playing-card from his pocket and, by the tip of his knife, was fashioning a snowflake. His hands were dead steady. His voice alone shook. "Ladies all up one wall and their mothers down the other. Devil I know why he does it."

The captain pressed his gloved knuckles under his eyes. "Because he is unwed and thirty-six, God save him."

"You've gone quite white," Linton added. He spoke to Captain Fleming as the inferior officer he had been, or a friend. "Puke in the coal-scuttle, if you've a mind to. Or go home, man. Half the men would bolt, it's tighter than a troop-ship—"

"I promised her I would. I—I thought I would speak to her."

"Ah. Speak to her?" Linton grinned, and it was not the grin of his grace the Earl's obedient servant. "Has she the sense God gave a marrow, she'll refuse you."

"I know it." *If she refuses, what have I to fear?*

Linton came close enough to brush the snow-melt from Fleming's shoulders, twist and coax his silver braid into better light against the blue. "Well. Maybe it's not so difficult, asking such a simple thing."

"It's not the asking. It's the telling."

"Beg pardon, Captain?"

"Said, you had better let me in, then."

Linton let him pass, without a word or a bow but with a solid shove in Fleming's back, for courage. In the spark and spill of candlelight, all the room was a momentary blur. Fleming had several heartbeats' time to think on the Provost Marshal, the pillory, Harriet's cut direct; she thought she had steel enough for all but the last.

"You look well," said Fleming, not much above a whisper. He did not give his back to the library threshold.

Harriet smiled at him. "One of the few delights of my years, Captain, is that I am no longer required to dress like a boiled sweet." She smoothed the skirt of her claret velvet gown and then took the chair the captain drew for her, that he might have something to do with his hands.

Fleming, for his part, struggled not to turn out his toes, or stand upon the outside of his boots; he was agonizing slow to pluck up conversation, now they were alone.

"Nathaniel—"

"Harry—"

Both faltered at once, and Harriet perhaps kicked the carpet. "I have missed you a great deal. Why you took yourself away so quickly after luncheon, I cannot venture."

Fleming closed his eyes a moment, as Sherbourne did when old wounds pained him, and when he spoke it did not ring quite the truth. "I wished to tell you—I wished," Fleming faltered, and then half lied. "Madam, I did not wish by my conduct to turn us into an *on dit*."

"Your conduct was most correct. You'd no reason to vanish from company like a ghost. And the hour is late for me to go compromising myself with cavalry-men!" Harriet glared, bright-eyed, at him. "If you would not have talk from my brother's guests, there is a simple expedient—quite aside from refraining to flee Sherry's town house while half of them are at Christmas lunch."

"I am coming to that—if making a mare's nest of it! I should have spoken last night. I *would* have, and let witness it who may." The captain dropped from his chair to his knees, and took up Harriet's hands. "Harry, I have near nothing in this world, save my honor and my sword."

Harriet did not draw away. She needed Fleming's grip, in any case, to keep from fainting to the carpet. His eyes were earnest and blue as ever, but not so steady as his hands.

"Harriet Georgiana, will you do me the great honor of becoming my wife?"

"I very much hoped you should speak your mind." She turned her face aside a moment. "You have mentioned it to my brother?"

"No," answered Fleming. "I—I thought his opinion no consequence in the matter."

Harriet laughed. "I accept you, then, Nathaniel, with all my heart."

He kissed her gloved fingers and bounded upright, smiling. "Shall we bring the news to him, dearest, and crown Twelfth Night as never before in this house?"

"Captain—Nathaniel—"

He paused in his stride, his smile never fading.

"In half an hour we shall go and tell Sherry he may wish me happy," said Harriet. "Until then, bear me company."

Fleming closed the library door. He came to her and kissed her; she had taken off her gloves, and her fingers slid and tangled in his hair. When he laid his lips to the pulse in her throat, Harriet shivered.

There was a reading-alcove to hand, hidden round by old, thick curtains, and Harriet pulled at the captain's shoulder until they fell, clinging together, into the cushions of its seat. Her curls were loose about Fleming, longer than he had known, and the curve of her breast above the red velvet was touched with attar of roses. The alcove was chill, but her hands upon him were afire, caught at the back of his breeches, pressing him desperate close.

"Harry…" Fleming meant to draw back, meant to heed the hammering blood as pleasure edged to panic. Harriet's teeth scraped toward Fleming's dolman collar, and her hands were—her hands—

Her hands flew from the front of the captain's breeches. Harriet screamed, and caught Fleming hard across the nose.

Eleanor leapt from the alcove seat, eyes blind and filling. "Harry," she got out, around the blood.

"Oh God." Harriet was curled half upon herself, biting her fingertips as she began to cry. "You are—you have been—all this *time!* Get off! Stand away!"

Eleanor had reached to comfort Harriet without thinking. "Harry, wait, cry you mercy!"

Harriet caught a ragged breath. "Oh God, I cannot bear it. You had my heart, and I was every moment deceived!"

"Please…"

"Get out."

"Please, listen!"

"We are at an end—sir—madam." Harriet had begun to collect herself; she jerked her bodice into place, and made her hands busy, rather than bury her face in them. "I do not consider you may entreat me to listen, or anything else."

"Dearest," said the captain, unwilling to give it over. She had taken her hand down from the shocking mess of her countenance, though she blinked and whitened still with pain; she seemed not to care for the blood upon her uniform. "I meant—I meant to tell you, sooner far than this."

Harriet was shaking, hard enough to mar her speech. "H-have I b-broken your nose?"

"Nicely," said Eleanor. She caught Harriet under the elbows, when she swayed, and set her down amidst the alcove's scattered cushions.

"*No,*" Harriet cried protest. "No! Take your hands away! Monster—viper—liar!"

Eleanor ducked under each word as if it were a blow. She gained the library door and opened it, her hand on the latch gone slippery with tears and blood. "Harry," she tried, low, for one last time.

"*Get out!*"

"Viscountess Beauchamp informs me you depart for Bournebrook."

"Sir, give you good evening." Harriet did not turn a hair at Eleanor's matched black eyes, badly gone over with a mottle of someone's powder.

"Viscountess Beauchamp rather delighted to inform me of it."

Harriet never smiled. "She is so very rarely right, sir; she must take her joy where she may. I fear she has played you false, all the same, and likely delighted the more."

"Madam?"

"I do not return to the Earl's house in Essex, sir."

Eleanor threw over courtesy. "Then where? Will you not give me your direction?"

Harriet cast her glance down to her shoes.

"May I not write to you for friendship's sake, if you insist on quitting London?"

"I fear it should be unwise to remain friends."

Eleanor clenched her fists hard enough to split her gloves. Then she bowed low over Harriet's hand, to make a brave show for the mob in the salon. "You hate me so much, then."

"I don't hate you. I don't know you." Harriet's voice cracked. "Captain, if you do not return to the entertainments, I fear Sherbourne's guests will begin to enquire. "

"Let 'em enquire—let them go to blazes." Eleanor drew a great breath and failed to check the pleading in her voice. "Harry, upon my word I am the same as you knew me yesterday."

"In all but a very few points." Harriet was polite, and dry, and cruel. "I do not care to know you as you were yesterday, when you made sport of a spinster on the shelf. Perhaps you will ask Sherbourne to marry you, today?"

"I wasn't making sport of you. I was thinking of your honor."

"My honor! Lord Jesus, Captain!"

"You knew what I meant," said Eleanor, beseeching. "Half London knows that we have carried on, Harry, as your cousin must hold forth upon every damn thing, and I asked you—I asked you because I love you!"

"Captain Fleming, you forget yourself!"

"I forget myself! *I!* I was not the one with her hand down my—oh, *shit*," Fleming swore out. Within, harp and piano jangled silent. One of Sherbourne's rather larger footmen came into the corridor and found the captain alone, wiping his streaming, stinging eyes, and covered from forehead to dress sword in crimson ratafia punch.

CHAPTER 10

The drive in Hyde Park was meant to fill the useless hours, to bleed the cold daylight away until Harriet could plead headache and retire to bed. In Sherbourne's well-appointed town house her cousin gamed Beauchamp's fortune away with avidity; the library was full of cigarillo-smoke and the racket of the faro machine, and Harriet found she could not bear society ladies of late. Of all Sherbourne's house-party, only Philomela Partington could be induced to accompany Harriet in the curricle, and Harriet had little enough upon which to speak to her. Philo was mad for gaming, indeed, and pined to be back at the house; but she had been obliged by her husband to abstain, having cost Lord Partington his rather fine shooting-lodge in Scotland.

In the near silence, Harriet froze by degrees. Sherbourne's town horses were grown elderly, so that he considered

Harriet might drive them herself; now as she listened to Philo natter upon the weather, Harriet's hands petrified in calfskin driving-gloves. The curricle's sway was lulling her to sleep.

"Oh, Harriet, look! Is that not your captain?"

"Dear Philo, he is not *my* anything."

He—*she* was handsome as the devil, her greatcoat flung back by the speed of her mount, breeches and waistcoat fitting with perfect deceit. The black horse, Harriet had not seen before, but it was delicate, dashing and quick; Fleming looked a highwayman. Her cheeks bore roses in the cold, one lock of golden hair had fallen forward, and her mouth…

There was nothing to remark about the captain's mouth. Harriet, for her part, bit the inside of her cheek.

"I say, Harriet, that horse much resembles Lord Uxbridge's Black Darnley! It cannot be his!"

"Not his," Harriet agreed, though the captain would have looked as well riding backward upon a jennet. "For speed I dare say it is Black Darnley, or one like him. Captain Fleming is much trusted in matters of horse-flesh."

"You mean to say he is *exercising* that horse, like any gentleman's groom?"

"His great pleasure is in riding," was all Harriet would say.

She kept her own team to the trot, and hoped for a bend in the path.

"Lady Beauchamp mentioned he was quite a member of the staff at Bournebrook. I wondered your brother permitted—but then he showed so very well in company, Harriet dear. I must say, though, he is dashed unfashionable for riding the Row! No crop to speak of, and no spur!"

"Captain Fleming does not hold with them."

"I know you must go along with him, of course. But—oh, Harriet—if you wished so very much to be married, surely you might have—"

"Philo, you're mistaken. I no longer wish to marry Captain Fleming."

"Oh, thank heaven! I do not think I could bear it. And Lady Beauchamp will be so much relieved. He seemed a very country sort of person, and she could not ascertain he had been to school at all! Though she did seem exceeding sure —" Philomela froze, the better to deliver her stage whisper with a *frisson* that might have carried to the Prince Regent's box at Covent Garden. "I hope you are not compromised, Harriet dear!"

Harriet might have let fly with half a dozen oaths to give her brother's company credit, but to her horror Captain Fleming had overtaken them.

"Whoa!" Fleming lifted her hat, but her expression bore no

pleasantry. "Whoa," she said again, to the black horse, and swung down into the road. "Your off horse has nearly cast a shoe. You must not drive on so—my lady Harriet, my lady Partington," she added, correct enough, but they might both have been dolls in a shop-window. "Let me help you down, if you please. I will have Darnley into harness as quickly I may, and walk Lord Sherbourne's beast."

"Lord Uxbridge's derby horse! I wonder you dare, sir!"

"My lord Uxbridge's signal concern is for a lady's safety. Had you rather turn over into the sand? Or…walk?" Captain Fleming did not quite match Lady Partington's rudeness. She came round to the driving side, and handed Harriet down.

"Unless you should rather not drive Darnley, madam?"

"What say you?" Having searched the captain's countenance for any message but plain concern, Harriet gave herself to the task at hand.

"Speak him fair and rein him firm, same as any silly child. I shan't let you come to harm."

Harriet nodded. She had kept hold of Fleming's hand, and even now could not let go, though nothing passed between them.

Philomela sneezed.

"Pray excuse me." Fleming cleared her throat. Then she

took off her greatcoat, cast it over the curricle seat, and went forward to the horses. Harriet could not help but watch her work. Philo moaned, near Harriet, of the spectacle they should make; the black racehorse and Lord Sherbourne's old roan, with a matched one limping behind, like a funeral. And in this cold!

"Do shut up, Philo!" Harriet snapped at last, and struck the curricle wheel. "Is all well, Captain?"

"All's well! Come and I'll show you…" Captain Fleming broke off, and her head went down out of sight by Black Darnley's flank. Harriet wished to weep.

The captain did not address her again until Lady Partington had been made snug, under Fleming's greatcoat, in the curricle, and the black racehorse had begun to stamp and test in the traces. She whispered, under the guise of offering Harriet her knee, "I thought you meant to leave London."

"I cannot abide Bournebrook in dead of winter," Harriet shrugged, as if every memory, every touch of Captain Fleming's hand slid off her. She could not keep it up. Her eyes blurred, her heart hammered, and worse, her hands were shaking; worst of all, when Fleming clasped them, Harriet leant forward and sobbed—once—into the captain's shirt.

"Madam." Fleming put her off, gently.

Harriet recovered herself, somewhat, before Philo could

lean out and stare. "You drive," she got out, without disaster.

"What?"

"Put me up on Strawberry. Pray you drive—I dare not."

"I have no saddle for him, and if the shoe—"

"If he throws the shoe, he will do it at a walk, for me as likely as you. I know how to ride, for God's sake!"

The captain bowed. Her face showed not the flicker of a smile. As if she moved a sack of meal, she did as Harriet bade. "People will stare," she warned, "at a woman astride in the Row."

"If you can bear it, why should not I?" Harriet could not find the wit to care if Philo heard.

HARRIET STOOD in the snow in Clarges Mews, shivering and stamping, until she could no longer feel her feet. She was still closer to Half Moon Street than the place she meant to be, but she could not make herself go forward. She looked down the corner as far as she could, but number thirty-nine, Clarges Street, was out of view.

Grooms were beginning to cross the mews, and somewhere near, an ash-pan was emptied over the area rails and banged clean for good measure, iron ringing upon iron in the cold.

The sun was quite up, and if she hoped for stealth, it was gone; she had slipped from the house in an old cardinal-cloak of her mother's, that her pelisse might not be seen missing, and twenty years in a cupboard had not faded it a jot. For a moment she gave herself over to the thought she might be recognized by someone of the *ton*, and then told herself the *ton* was jolly well still asleep, half of them in Sherbourne's guest bedrooms. *Surely it is not calling upon a gentleman if you do it before his milk-seller,* Harriet told herself, and half-slid, half-splashed down the street.

Number thirty-nine's door had a scar upon it from the corn-law riots. It had weathered to a wet gray against the black paint, and a crack chased its way from the gash in the wood to where the knocker would have been, if anyone who cared for fashion was at home. The stucco housefront was still near the same gray as the rest of the row, but pieces had started to fall round the windows, showing plain outmoded brick. Snow was heavy as fleece upon the stairs. If she mounted them, she would be wet to the shins on a moment.

Harriet took them clumsily indeed, but she gained the door. Then she drew a deep breath and could not knock.

When the door opened, Harriet shrieked and nearly tumbled into the street.

"I ought really to hang the knocker, but dash it to hell, I can't find it."

"C-captain!"

Fleming looked unslept, her hair loose and her frock-coat swinging open over an old cavalry coverall. She made half a pass at straightening up, and went into rather a sarcastic bow. "I passed you in the mews ten minutes since, madam, but you seemed intent on your affairs. You had better come in; I have cut toast enough, and the coffee is still hot."

It was not the scene Harriet had pictured. She stepped over the threshold into the dimness, and it was not, either, how she had pictured that. The woman she had known as Nathaniel Fleming was not at her elbow—was, in fact, half down the corridor and indifferent—and Harriet herself was sharpish close to tears.

The downstairs parlour was bright, and the fire was good. A pair of high, hobnailed boots was steaming dry at the fender, and a cloak hung from the chimney-corner with rather a smell of wet horse. At the height of Harriet's eye, upon the wall, a faded god chased a faded nymph; further on, one of them had changed into a column of cloud, or a tree. The black-and-white Holland tiles shifted and clicked a bit beneath Harriet's feet, but the floor was shining clean.

"Pray you be seated, Lady Harriet."

"Miss Fleming," she replied, still standing; but she could not keep up the style. "Captain—Nathaniel—oh, God rot it," Harriet said, "I do not even know your Christian name."

"I think that is as well, madam."

"I should like to have it." Harriet persisted. "There are… things I have come to say."

Perched upon the edge of the most distant sofa, the captain gave her familiar forward shrug, coming to rest with her elbows on her knees.

"Please—"

"Christened Eleanor. Called Nora. What have you come to say, then?"

Harriet paced. She had taken off her gloves and wrung them, but it did not help her speak. "I think…I think I must be in love."

"Give you joy of it," said Eleanor. "I had rather you threw the coffee at me."

"No, Nora, I meant—"

Eleanor neither moved nor spoke, but something like hope mingled with exhaustion in her face.

"It is love, I think, when a person sends you mad as Bedlam, and yet without them you have no gladness and no rest?"

"Madam, if you are in love with a half-pay army captain, I must advise you let it go."

"I will throw him over on the moment," said Harriet false-lightly. "If I might have you instead."

∽

"TELL ME THE TRUTH?" Harriet asked. They were stretched before the big, outmoded hearth in Fleming's tiny study; Eleanor lay with her head on Harriet's lap, and Harriet had smoothed Eleanor's bright hair out into a fan.

"What would you have me tell you?"

"Dearest," said Harriet, ""I want to know everything, all, from true life, not from ballads."

"Everything, all?" Fleming repeated, but trailed off humming *Polly Oliver*, because she did not know where to begin.

"What sort of girl were you, before?"

The girl by the graves was freezing, mist sticking her mother's black sarsnet gown against her skin. The sleeves were too short and the skirt was too long, and the bodice flapped loose until she crossed her arms. Her hat had gone, in a wrench of pins, half through the service, and the moor-wind had tangled her long pale hair all in hopeless knots. She was wearing a grown woman's shoes—she was a woman grown—and spoiling the blue-black silk with bloodied blisters.

"Colly, what will we do?"

Her eldest brother—newly Sir Colquhoun—was in his Cambridge chambers. She had thought all the week, as the bodies lay in the buttery, that the letter had gone astray. Then he had made answer, on a black-edged card with a gaudy gilt wafer: See to it, Nora.

"I suppose I was the sort of girl you get when your father has three sons before you and knows you only to hand your pin-money on quarter days. I read everything my brothers did, and better, and quite usurped the music-master; I was exceeding happy, for a female."

She was not quite alone in the house. There was Hiram Sloane, to stand as groom and footman and butler, and Mrs. Hiram Sloane, for the cook and charwoman's part. There had not been a governess or a lady's maid at Moorlowe since the death of Lady Fleming; Nora was grown used to sprinkling gowns and crimping pie-crusts for Mrs. Hiram Sloane, currying horses and carrying water at need. Lately her father's brother, his man of business, had come to look over Colquhoun's estate. He gave Nora five minutes' nonsense upon riding astride as unsuited to a gently bred woman; she looked at the ceiling and traced the dried-amber skitter of a leak from the roof. He boxed her ears, once each, and now he kept to her father's rooms and she must endure him only at dinner.

"My first brother is at Moorlowe with the title," Eleanor said. "Reynard died when my mother did—when I was twelve. Nathaniel—I must have been sixteen."

"Oh, Nora, how awful."

"He was…he wanted so very much to go for a soldier. My father bought the commission, and he and Nate both were in coffins before the ink had dried."

With pen-hand shaking she scratched the quill end again, and again, and again over Nate's death-lines, until all the ink and sand had flaked away clean. She shook the quarto and blew the truth away. Then she wrote, with exceeding care and flourish, Eleanor Charlotte Fleming, Anno aetatis suae Sixteene, keeping the magistrate's misspelling. She crept from her father's study and into the corridor soft as the dead.

"So you took it up in his stead," said Harriet. "Why on earth, Nora?"

She was fast and small and she could fight; she cracked her forehead against his, caught his breastbone with an elbow, and shoved. Her uncle's hand was no longer cold as an eel down her bodice.

"You ought to be killed," he sputtered. His nose was pouring blood. Her last gown was ruined.

Eleanor ran. She shut herself into the first chamber with a good lock upon the door, turned the key and lent the oaken door the strength of her back. It was Nate's room, the bedstead empty, the curtains burned and the naked windows showing starlight; it smelled still of ambergris and a young man's pomade. Haphazard upon the desk were a sabre and a bicorne and Nate's discarded pocket. His chests and his armoire were full.

"I was, God, I was weary of fever-nursing. It seemed I had done it for years, and for nothing. So *I cut my locks and I changed my name*, and there it was."

She was two hours upon the road to London, riding flat out, when someone behind hailed. "Whoa, Miss Nora, Miss Nora!"

Hiram Sloane, stained and sweated from riding 'cross country, lumbered his great gelding up into the road. The horse was pack-laden as if for a journey, bundles near to spilling in the moonlight. The sabre she had abandoned—she did not know how to use it—gleamed silver where it was tied to Hiram Sloane's cantle.

"Miss Nora—Master Nate—you have forgot your arms, and your letter of commission!"

"I had my seventeenth birthday at Benavente, pissed myself in the saddle, and should have deserted; but I had to run about stealing horses for my lieutenant, as he *would* keep getting them shot from under him."

"To think you knew Sherry, so long ago!"

Fleming shrugged. "I was not his friend, not truly, until much later. When I met him I should only have said, *I see why they follow him*, and I did the same."

HARRIET OPENED her eyes in the last watch of night. There was rushlight in the room, and over and around her face there spilled a glory of gold. She blinked full awake, shook herself free and stretched; she smiled and could not stop smiling. Her ankle brushed over Eleanor's bare calf.

Eleanor sat up, alert, bewildered; the edge of her hand came just short of Harriet's throat.

"Nora?!"

"Harry. Oh, Christ," she said sadly. "I am too much a soldier."

Harriet twined her fingers through Eleanor's, finding a bit of her smile again. "*Give ye good morning* is more usual, in the peace," she said, to steady them both.

"Good morning; it isn't quite four." Eleanor turned aside to twitch the rushlight. The moment's brightness showed the sharp mark above her breasts where linen had drawn too tightly.

"Nora," began Harriet, and did not know the words to continue. She touched Eleanor instead, half to please, half to comfort.

"The least of half a dozen hurts, dearest, and the one I'm most used to. I am old, you know."

Harriet stuck out her tongue. In the wild light she dared look longer at Eleanor than she did even clothed, in daylight. There were marks she knew, sabre cuts and old leather-burns on fingers and wrists, but most of her scars had gone hidden. The long silver line on Eleanor's right forearm, *Genappe*, the round-and-jagged dip in her left shoulder, *Orthez*. Harriet drew the bedclothes back and Eleanor flinched, one knee tucking to her chest, just as the light smoked and dropped.

"Mend the light?"

"We might as easily leave it out."

"Mend it," Harriet insisted. "One hears, madam, that lovers sometimes regard one another."

"Madam, I have never had the leisure."

The dressing-table was too far to reach; Harriet struck her tongue on her teeth and leant over Eleanor, then threw herself over Eleanor's knee when she could not find the rush by touch. She burned her fingertips and cursed.

"I shall spend my bride-price on candles," said Harriet, "and look at you all I like. Stop *gloating.* I'm *singed.*"

For apology, Eleanor drew Harriet's burned forefinger into her mouth.

"Oh." The air around them was suddenly thick to breathe, and Harriet went dizzy. She shivered, because the air touched her skin, because Eleanor's skin did; she wanted a thousand things at once. "Oh, Nora."

She said it over and again, without knowing whether she soothed or summoned. She laid her tongue upon every scar she could find, and when she must breathe it was *Nora*; she learnt her way while the light lasted, kissed the inside of Eleanor's knee and upward until Eleanor thrashed, begged, whimpered, and *Nora,* Harriet murmured, all of a piece with *yes* and *mine* and *for me.*

Time had gone from her head. She was teasing tremors from Eleanor's inner thigh when the rushlight hissed and sent them into darkness; Harriet, made bold, twisted to brace Eleanor's legs upon her shoulders. She stilled, with Eleanor's pulse beating mad against her ear.

"Harry!"

She cast a steadying hand over Eleanor's hip and pressed forward; thought one shocking clear moment of her salvation, and darted out her tongue.

THE DOOR WOULD REND from its hinges in half a moment. "Cap, oi, Captain Sir! Pray wake, and look sharp!"

Eleanor was waking. She reached beside the bed and hurled what came to hand, a lady's shoe; on a moment the rattle and pounding ceased.

"I am—Cornet, I am indisposed!"

"Beg pardon, Captain, only it's the major, and he's that drunk. I cannot shift him."

"Ten minutes," she gasped. "Saddle Malabar and the major's Kestrel, if we must go and rescue the princess!"

Beside her upon the camp bed, a protest went muffled into the pillows.

"Only I mislike to wake Queen Mab, Captain, she's snappish in the dark…"

"I'll give thee snappish, lad, damn 'ee for a nuisance!"

Cornet Blakeney retreated, at speed and in fear; Eleanor turned to lay conciliatory kisses anywhere Sabine would allow.

"C'est bullshit!"

"I know," she replied, raking her hair into a painful queue. "I'm terribly sorry. Wait for me, if you may?"

She knew it would be empty quarters on her return. With a mutinous pout, Sabine turned to the wall. "Why must you go at all?"

"Because it would shame the regiment were he to die in his own sick." Eleanor scowled. Her nerves were unspooled to the edges, and when Sabine touched her naked back Eleanor jumped.

"I suppose you must dress."

"Hard luck on the village if I didn't," Eleanor answered, set her feet on the freezing floor, and reached for her coverall and shirt.

"Arms up." Sabine was deft by now with Fleming's bandages, wrapping the first layers even before Eleanor had clasped her hands behind her head.

"Thank you." The last of desire had given way to duty as Sabine fastened Eleanor's sleeves and her coverall braces. Sabine knelt, wrapped in Fleming's army blanket, with her dark hair falling round her; she gave several critiquing touches at the coverall's front buttons.

"You make really a fetching man, you know."

"Merci, mignonne," said Eleanor and kissed her, but it little comforted her when she had closed the door.

Blakeney was below, with the horses, sulking against one of Sherbourne's mounts in the cold. He wore his pelisse straight on, and a greatcoat over all; he held Fleming's horse with a hand gone blue and red.

"Your gloves, cornet?"

"Sir!" He stood straight, if not tall. "Lost them, Cap, Sir."

"If the lieutenants take your uniform, tell the major," she said. She had said it before. "You are not obliged to punch them, but you are obliged to keep your kit." Eleanor crouched on the frozen ground and gave the boy hand and knee, tossing him up to the saddle, then peeled her own gloves off and handed them to Blakeney.

"I will have a shilling out of you every quarter-day," she promised. "See you keep those; they belong to the King."

"Aye, Captain."

"It is as well you came to fetch me," Eleanor said, when they were upon the road. "I have wanted a word."

"With me, Sir?"

"Concerning your conduct." She drew a breath shocking cold, and did not hedge. "You must break it off with Captain Fraser."

"Why, would you have me come to you instead? Are you upon the outs with Major Sherbourne?"

Eleanor let out a whoop. She folded over her pommel, kicked in her stirrups, and bashed her forehead on Malabar's startled neck. "Major Sherbourne!" *She cried.* "Art'a daft as a brush, Cornet!"

"…What?"

"Have you run mad, young sir," said Eleanor, slowly and with diction. "To suggest Major Sherbourne takes liberties with my person, or I with his!"

Blakeney hunched away, as far as he could without losing balance as they rode abreast. "You need not give me lies," he muttered. "All the squadron knows you are sodomites."

Still shaking and gasping with laughter suppressed, Eleanor reached to clap his shoulder. "Upon—upon my word, Cornet, the squadron is wrong. Mine nor the major's cards fall out that way."

"C-Captain Fraser says you ought to have risen lieutenant-colonel— but you do not wish to leave the major. And you are ever in his tent before engagements!"

"Conning maps, lad, or am I meant to be buggering Exploring Officer Kent as well? He is rather often present." Eleanor swallowed the last of her mirth, and said more gently, "A hundred men's lives are enough for me to bear. When you are older, you may find it so."

"You are not in love with him, then, truly?"

"No, my hand upon the Testament."

"Then you cannot understand about Jack and me!"

Eleanor sighed. "Must I give an order, Cornet Blakeney? Quite omitting to take your skin off for speaking him Jack in my hearing."

"Give any order you like. I will not leave off with him. I cannot."

"If you cannot leave off, resign your commission and go home to England, and shame your mother the less! If Fraser has coerced you—"

"No!"

"Captain Fraser has a wife but lately returned to London." Eleanor watched his body tense. "He does not love her, if that comforts you, but never a moment think that he will leave her." She tapped Blakeney's stirrup with her boot. "It is my duty to break your heart to save your neck," she said, low. "If you make your name as a Ganymede, it will not go easy for you."

He was still young enough to look always gangling and hungry; sketched in her night-vision, the cornet's countenance was like a knife. "It is too late for that, upon my word! The lads—from the beginning, even before—"

"Thrash 'em," said Eleanor, promptly. "Or send 'em to Sherbourne for thrashing, or myself. The army is no place to be a gentleman."

"Captain," said Blakeney at last, and if he sniffled into his collar, the night was cruelly chill. "What shall I do?"

"Go to Fraser's quarters—I will give you some nonsense to carry—and say he must give you up, because you would not see him hang."

"Hang!"

"Jesus, lad!" Eleanor thought she should have to catch the boy before he brained himself in the road. Cornet Blakeney kept his seat, just, but she braced his near shoulder all the same.

"I did not know—I did not believe—what's that?"

There was a hummock in the road ahead. It was indistinctly shaped, well-muffled, and it was singing.

"Some come here to fiddle and dance, some come here to tarry! Some come here to fiddle and dance, I came here to...marry!"

"We have found the major," said Eleanor, and dropped from the saddle without catching Blakeney's glance.

CHAPTER 11

"*A* word in private, Sherry?"

"Go on, then." Sherbourne hauled his game leg up to toast before the fender. "Drink, will you?"

"Thank you, no."

"Speak your mind, old Spaniel. This isn't a campaign tent."

Eleanor stood at parade rest notwithstanding, to keep from clasping arms behind her back and scuffing her boot-toe in patterns along the carpet. "Sherry," she began, and failed. "I'm not young—"

She swallowed and wished she had taken him up on strong drink.

"…Holy hell, you haven't a *tendre* for me, have you?"

Sherbourne eyed the captain. "I've changed my mind. Hold your tongue!"

She stared back, and decided to get it over at once before things got thicker. "Major, I should like to speak for your sister's hand in marriage."

"Good God, man! Is she increasing?"

Eleanor fell back a pace at the snarl of his gaze. He had eyes very like Harriet's, she thought, but they threatened her ruin for reasons entirely apart. "Upon my word, no."

Sherbourne subsided. "You gave me a fright, Spaniel. Marry my sister!"

"Sherry, I am in earnest."

"You can't afford her, lad! Or she can't afford you, much the same thing. I love her dear as life, but Pater left precious little in the estate; she's only got two hundred pounds a year. And b'God I know what you draw."

"We have spoken on that account."

"Think what a life it will be for her, following the drum."

Eleanor winced. "You know very well, sir, I shall not be fit for action again."

"You've gone skittish because it's peace, and peace is deuced boring. Never mind this nonsense of *sir* and *Major*. If the King called you—hell, if *I* called you—"

"Then I should invalid out of the regiment, Sherry, and draw a pension fit to keep your sister."

"And until then, shall you rub along nicely on bread and water in that pile in Clarges Street, with the roof that knew Cromwell when he had his head?"

"I swear she will not know want, Sherry, and if I have little enough on the bank, at least she will have my honor and my name."

"Oh, hell," said Sherbourne. "You mean to keep on with this!"

"I mean only to have your answer."

"She's clever, Fleming, You don't want clever. It's nothing but a trial. You're a beau yet, you've a war-wound, one turn round the floor at Almack's and you could beat them off with sticks—"

Eleanor lifted her chin.

"Don't," Sherbourne put up his hands as if to meet a punch. "Don't, Spaniel. Take her if you want her! But don't give me a word about devotion, or love. Not from you! I can't bear it."

"…Sherry?"

"Take her, I said. Write to Bournebrook church and have the banns called. Write to my man of business; there's a ring. Write to Mother, damned if I shall do it. And I suppose

Harriet must have some damned-fool party, and empty the town of champagne. See to it, Spaniel."

She legged him a bow. "Thank you, Sherry. With all my heart—"

"Oh, get stuffed!"

SHE HAD GROWN adept at creeping from her brother's house. Plundering the kitchens Harriet was less sure of, and trade at such an hour could only be done in ready money, so the breakfast was not what she could have wished. Still there was a pot of chocolate, half a dozen currant cakes, and an eggworth of butter wrapped in grease-paper; and in her reticule, clinking against the coins, was Fleming's spare front-door key.

There was no sign of life on the first floor, only the wind down the chimney stirring the dust of a cold fire. It was eerie to see Eleanor's parlour without the warm clutter of her presence; the faded figures upon the walls were not friendly, and the étagères at the room's edges seemed waiting for some soul fifty years gone to return and pick up this curio, that ammonite. Harriet did not linger, even to take off her cloak.

Eleanor was asleep, bedclothes cast wildly round her, and never stirred when Harriet set down her basket. Harriet drummed upon the box-bed's panels, softly; Eleanor rolled further into the pillows.

"Nora. Nora, dearest!" Harriet stepped from her shoes and climbed into the bed. She fit herself under the topmost quilt, slid her arm along the warm angle of Eleanor's hip, and waited.

Eleanor woke from the absence of a dream. There was a familiar tickle of curls against her collar, and welcome heat and softness at her back.

"Harry," she said, and turned to her for a kiss. "How came you here?"

"Afoot, and an hour ago." Harriet sat away, giving her best to look stern. "You've slept passing late. Will you be missed in the Row?"

"I had set today aside for diverse purposes," Nora answered. "A lie-in not least. But I do think it is the law in England," she went on, drawing Harriet back down to her by the wrists. "A gentleman may avail himself twenty minutes on Tuesdays for tumbling such ladies as sneak into his chamber."

"Twenty minutes!" Harriet scoffed. "Time enough for a gentleman, maybe. And I never snuck—sneaked. I am possessed of your house-key, and I am saint enough to bring your breakfast."

"Are not you the breakfast, madam?"

"Madam, cease," Harriet answered, "Or I will quit the room."

Eleanor cast her hands to the pillows, smirk spreading to a grin. "Stand away, then."

Harriet kept her seat. She pushed Eleanor's nightshirt high as she could, baring stomach, ribs, breasts to her touch while Eleanor fought at the sea of linen; she warmed her fingertips against Eleanor's nipples until, beneath her, Nora cried out and could not be still.

"How anyone mistook you a man, once you were abed with them," Harriet said softly, wadding the nightshirt to toss away, "I declare I have no idea."

"Was not—pray don't stop—abed with many, and all knew hart from hind!"

Harriet froze.

Eleanor opened her eyes, and after a pained moment covered them with her hands. She breathed out in a hard rush. "Dearest, I meant you no—"

"I'm not," said Harriet. "They knew? Women. And—you knew. That they." The weight of her body slipped from Eleanor's thighs. She looked mazy, trying once and again to speak. "How?"

"How did you know your eyes are dark?" Eleanor gave a question for answer.

"I… I must have looked in the glass, when I was small."

She sat up, drawing Harriet near. "It is very like looking in a glass, to me. Something you see without remarking it—something you know because it is so in yourself."

"If you should be wrong?"

"One is only wrong once, generally." Eleanor softened it with half a smile.

"And you saw—that—in me?"

"I saw you, and thought I would risk the rest."

"Do you think I could do that?"

Eleanor paused in tying her maharatta, and gave a strange look to Harriet by the glass.

"Not tie your cravats. Go as a man, I meant."

"I knew." Eleanor put her head on one side. "What for? You've no need to draw pay, or court women—I guess—and I mislike to think you might go for a sailor."

"To see what it might be like," replied Harriet, and more firmly when Fleming recoiled, "Not for sport. To know what it must feel like, to be—you."

Eleanor finished her knot before she spoke. "It is not a good idea, Harry."

"I only—"

"You do not mean to go guising for sport, I know. But it is harder than it looks, dearest, and I could not bear it if—"

"If I made a cake of myself in public?"

"If you should end in the pillory!"

Harriet moved where she might comfort Eleanor by touch, though she shuddered herself. "I was not making light, dearest."

Eleanor shrugged. "Somewhere up here be rigs I wore when I was younger. They are out of the style, but they might do you for a masque."

"I have no wish whatever to masquerade a boy! It is your life, and so mine, and I would understand!" Harriet stamped her foot.

Eleanor might have smiled, behind her hand. "Stow that, for a start."

Half an hour later, she sat upon the tea-table to get the best point of view, hopping down now and again to twist, or tug, or cuff at Harriet's clothes. "Stand, really stand," she ordered. "Take up the room! You are an Englishman! If your back does not hurt, and your heels, and your shoulders, you've failed. Point your chin at the chimney-piece!"

"You mean to give me no quarter at this," said Harriet, hopping out of reach in the unfamiliar boots.

"None," Eleanor agreed, seizing Harriet's shoulders and hauling her back before the glass. "God Jesus, talk so I might hear you. Men are heard, Harry, always!"

Harriet, in a young man's bottle-green cutaway and fawn waistcoat and a well-braced pair of Eleanor's breeches, slumped somewhat. "You are right," she said. "I am quite a loss."

"God, no, fetching rather…though the upper storey is a problem."

Harriet crossed her arms upon her chest. "Why do you shout so at me, then?"

"I'm not shouting, dearest. Only speaking you as I might Sherry, or any lad who knew me by Christian name."

"I think I am addled in the mind," Harriet said. "May I not sit?"

"Don't know," answered Eleanor. "Not my business telling a gentleman what he may do."

Harriet dropped straight down onto the floor. A waistcoat-button flew. "The upper storey, indeed!"

"Malign it not too much."

"But what am I to do?"

Eleanor crouched beside her, tracing her knuckle down Harriet's nose. "Go on, if you like; or give over. I am your servant, madam, even though you go off hare-brained."

Harriet bit Eleanor's lip. "Hare-brained! What if I should want to dress like this always?"

"Then we must to Paris, and a tailor," said Eleanor, closing another kiss, but utterly grave. "It could be done, if you wished. Hellish, though—hellish morning and night. It is not what I should want for you, dearest."

"You manage."

"I have not your…graces," blushed Eleanor.

"I own I find nothing lacking in yours. I should like to go on, please," said Harriet, tilting up her chin.

Eleanor sat with her boots planted square, elbows on knees, chin on wrists. She might not have heard a thing.

"I'll go on." Harriet jumped to hear her voice ring off the walls, the furniture, her own frame. She was hot, and sore, and the short words were pitched with temper.

"As you like, lad," said Eleanor, and lent her a hand up.

All the binding linen Eleanor had to spare was stiff with newness, and she drew it with no little strength, though she was quick from long practice and gentler with Harriet than herself. Harriet clasped her hands in her hair, studied the ceiling, and only at the last let any noise past her teeth.

"*Ow!*"

"Arms down," said Eleanor, and stroked Harriet's back as if to make amends. "I did tell you…"

"I can't breathe," said Harriet, nothing like a boy, as Eleanor helped her on with shirt, waistcoat, and cutaway all again. "Nora, how can you breathe?"

"Much shouting," she answered, "and much singing. Say something."

"Say *what*?"

"Say 'God save the King.'"

Harriet echoed it, plucking all the while at her waistcoat front.

"No! Upon my word. He is the King. He is mad as Nero Augustus, and he will have you taken from your sweetheart, and stuffed into a troop-ship, and order you must face the foe and die! You very much wish him saved, and that well away from you!"

"God save the King," said Harriet, bolder, and felt it where Eleanor's hand lay upon her stomach.

"If you come over faint, fold in half, touch your boots, and say 'God save the King.'" Eleanor tweaked at Harriet's binding. "Don't ask me. I learnt it second-hand. If you feel queer in the street, set your back to a wall and look foxed. No one pays any mind."

"In the street!"

"You don't imagine I should hide so comely a boy in my rooms?"

"I am no wise ready to put to the test," Harriet whispered.

"You look passing better in your brother's hat than does your brother." Eleanor set a brown velvet coachman over Harriet's curls. To what Harriet had spoken, she said nothing. "You want a set of side-whiskers, but it's as well. I can't abide to be tickled."

Eleanor stood away, leaving Harriet in the center of the chamber. Harriet could not see a boy in the glass, however she stood and lifted her chin. She swung her arms and rocked in her boots, and then tried to stand as Eleanor did, at rest; she looked, to herself, a badly-strung puppet.

"Remember you are an Englishman," said Eleanor. "A gentleman! I mean to take you no unsafe place, but if you remember that, you will buy yourself less trouble. And— remember I am with you."

"And armed to the teeth," Harriet remarked, with a stab at keeping her voice low. "Where do you mean to take us?"

"Oh, Bevis Marks," said Eleanor.

"To Aldgate—among the Jews!" She forced her hand away from her mouth. It was not a gesture Eleanor would make.

"Nowhere a man might fear to go."

CHAPTER 12

The shop was signed only by a gilt ball, hanging on a fanciful wroughtwork curlicue over the street. Its windows were small and diamond-paned, and candles burned in them as though it was not broad day.

"Splendid, a day for business." Eleanor quickened her step. "It's luck; I can never remember when their Sunday might be."

Harriet, loping in unfamiliar boots, was a stride behind now Eleanor did not match pace with a lady. She came under the jeweler's awning all blown, wiping perspiration from forehead and hatband, and could not quite manage to make her waistcoat lie smooth. She had made no acquaintance with Jews, but their shopfronts and their shop's-bells were the same; she flattened back against Eleanor, a bit, lest the interior show something outlandish or untoward, but under the sign of the golden ball was a jeweler's like any in Mayfair.

"Come down, Elie, it is Lady Linley's granddaughter the captain!" There was a woman behind the counter, running a cloth over the dustless glass of locked jewel-cases. She was smaller than Harriet, and rounder, but her voice was not timid.

"They know, then!" Harriet meant it for a whisper.

"Mendelssohn was my grandmother's man for her jewels," Eleanor answered. "I have known the father and the son—Mr. Mendelssohn present—since my hair was in plaits. When Grandmamma—when I no longer came here in her company, it did not sit well to start a lie."

"We had an eye upon the casualty lists, Captain, after Bonaparte was sent down, and were most grateful you had been sustained—but I declare we have not seen you since!"

"My regiment was held to keep the peace at Paris," said Eleanor. "I am only arrived in Town September past."

"I suppose you may be excused, then. Eliezer, faster is better!"

Harriet was unused to being invisible to men—women—of trade; she felt gaudy and small in her bottle-green coat. The jeweler's wife came from behind the counter, to greet Fleming French-fashion, and held her bare hand out for Harriet's kiss.

"Miri Mendelssohn," she said. "You are a friend of the forgetful Captain Fleming…?"

Eleanor coughed. "Harry—Lady Harriet—let me make you known to Mrs. Mendelssohn. Mrs. Mendelssohn, the Lady Harriet Sherbourne."

Mrs. Mendelssohn exclaimed, and drew her hand back before Harriet could grasp it. "Captain, why did you not say you were on real business? I will fetch him down at once!"

"All the business is mine, I am afraid, small as it is." Eleanor smiled. "I am content to wait him, if my lady—?"

Harriet had turned to con over one of the glass-topped cases. She looked up from the pendants and stickpins and nodded. "It will give me time to say which of these suits you," she said. "You had nothing from me at New Year's."

"I am not one for frippery, Harry…"

"These are beautiful things—some quite old," answered Harriet. "The old ones are not frippery. And your neckcloth needs something; you have no pin I know of, and you forever tie the same."

"I did not know you made a study." Eleanor was beginning to go pink. She was extricated, before Mrs. Mendelssohn could open the case for Harriet, by loud creaks of the swaying staircase as someone came below.

He had hair red as an Irishman's, and eyes hazel-green

behind a gold pince-nez, and a flattened round cap like a tonsure upon his head. He bore the look, as Sherbourne, of a man who had crossed the Rubicon of thirty-five and settled to better filling out his waistcoat. He grinned when he saw Eleanor, and bowed with flourishing wrist.

"You are aging well, Madam Captain."

"Bless all such lies, Mr. Mendelssohn; I will give you the same."

On rising from his courtesy, the jeweler had noticed Harriet; now he took her measure frankly, from her boots to the crown of her coachman's hat, until Eleanor cleared her throat.

"Eli, I should like to see the Linley pieces, please."

"Another horse, is it?"

"No, I thank you, Malabar does well."

"You must need a pair for Town driving, there's the way of it!"

"Upon my word, I am not come into fortune," Eleanor laughed. "Only—a happy chance. I thought to give Lady Harriet her choice among what's left."

Mr. Mendelssohn's eyebrows rose, but he spoke no question. He bowed again, and with his wife, disappeared. He returned alone, in a moment, carrying a box ostentatiously locked, with a gilt-figured key.

"Madam Captain," he said, and set the box down for Fleming to open it.

He unrolled a piece of clean velvet, showing upon it a chatelaine of filigree gold, a brooch set with cracked coral and milky-green jade, and four or five pendants with stones. There was a signet, too, its cuts softened by age at the edges, but the gold still bright; Eleanor tossed it aside like a pebble.

"I would like to see that one, please." Harriet closed her hand upon the signet.

"It is a man's ring, lady, and I could not bring it to proportion without damage to the intaglio."

Harriet examined its design, a plain shield of arms bearing a thistle bloom, but more carefully she looked to Eleanor's face.

"I will have nothing, if you do not have this."

"I don't—"

"You do want it, very much, or you should not have put it from you like that—and it belongs to you, besides!"

"Belonged to my grandfather Linley," she said. "And I am not of consequence enough to require a seal."

"You are—or you will be, when we have wed."

"Harry—"

"I don't think you had better cross her, Captain," the jeweler said. "I will take your lady's measure while you come to grips. And I will do the work gratis upon that ring, if it ease you!"

"Mendelssohn, don't gloat. It looks as though you've come over bilious."

The jeweler came round the counters again. He divested Harriet of her gloves and felt her finger-joints, and measured them with a thread that seemed quite ordinary. He passed a tape round Harriet's neck, but made note of the result by no means Harriet could see; he made no comment upon her mode of dress. He bent to her, instead, as if to learn the thickness of her cravat, and so spoke into her ear.

"I would you did not sport with the captain upon marriage. She is too good to be so used."

"You dare!" He was a tradesman and a Jew; she need not give him more, and yet she flinched when he did.

"I beg your pardon, madam; it is all very well for you to play a game of flats, but my friend could lose her commission—I daresay her life. I but attempt to dissuade you continuing so for amusement."

"I have accepted Captain Fleming's addresses," Harriet replied, more loudly than she intended. Fleming started up from her elbow-loll on the frame of one of the cases.

"All's well, Harry?"

"Quite well," she said, and smiled.

"My lady Harriet was sketching me your acquaintance," said Mr. Mendelssohn. "As you are appalling with the pen, and never graced us to know you courted."

"I have done courting," Eleanor corrected. "Now, by grace, I must only keep her, and she seems willing."

"Nora!"

"Do you mean to make her known to Mrs. Hannaford?" Mr. Mendelssohn was gathering up the Linley jewels, arranging and tying their velvet bundle, and carried the cask away again perhaps without notice of Eleanor's silence.

"Mrs. Hannaford? I never heard of such a person. What did the Jew mean?"

Eleanor tilted her head to Harriet. "He has a Chri—a given and a surname, when last I saw his mark."

"Mr. Mendelssohn, then," said Harriet.

"He was having sport of me, but certainly I might do so. Not in those clothes, I think," she added, "I fear you would be mistaken for the dessert."

THERE WERE two well-dressed men at a game of cards, and another in the corner with a note-book and pen.

"It is always so quiet, at the Season," said Mrs. Hannaford. "A score more will come, at perhaps ten o'clock, when the Runners make their presence known in the park."

Eleanor had gone to greet the young gentleman with the ink-blotted cuffs; Harriet, alone, shrank down between the door and Mrs. Hannaford's panniered hip. Nora might have been gone half a minute, but it felt an hour.

"Let me make you known to Mary and Grace, who have been called to Lords these twenty years by other names, and Olivia St. Clair, who writes for Ackerman's." Mrs. Hannaford nudged Harriet upon the room as though she were a wallflower at a country dance. "This is—upon my word, what will we call her? This lady is Captain Nathaniel Fleming's intended."

"Your intended! Captain, you do not play for halves!"

"Comes of her failure to die in pieces at Waterloo."

Eleanor shrugged. "I fell in love. She said she would have me."

Harriet had not colored so fiercely since her coming out. "Nora," she whispered, and would have addressed those assembled, but she had no idea what to say.

"Hold hard a moment, madam, I know you! Your father was—"

"My father was no man of consequence," Harriet cut the gentleman.

"Oh, now! Have you given our Fleming the lie? Step softly, Captain, this is an earl's daughter!"

Eleanor, easy as breathing, had her sabre half unsheathed. "Have a care how you speak the lady, Mary. Unlike yourself, I've something in my hanger."

"Mother! *Mother,* she has drawn arms upon me!"

"Captain," Mrs. Hannaford called from the top of the room. "Stop menacing the girls. Sit you to the pianoforte, and stay out of trouble."

Eleanor looked reluctant to give up Harriet's side.

Harriet astonished herself and let go Nora's arm, with a kiss. "Do. You have not played since…" All her sudden courage was lamed by memory. "Since Sherry's party."

Eleanor bowed toward Mrs. Hannaford, but her smile was for Harriet, and real. "What will you have, dearest?"

"Oh, Captain, will you not give us *Rambling Soldier?*" The man Eleanor had called Grace, resplendent in a frock-coat of peony pink, spoke out before Harriet could.

"I will give it to you in exchange for *The Butterfly,*" Eleanor replied. "I have scarcely danced with my intended, and I want something rather nicer than cotillions."

"And how," drawled Grace, "am I to strip the willow with your wife if I am fiddling?"

"Life goes hard." Eleanor fixed her countenance very grave.

"Oh, Lord! I am a martyr to a decent singing-voice. I'll take your price. When you are not in Town, we must all listen to St. Clair's poetry."

"Suck my prick," cried she in answer, and did not lay down her pen.

When every candle had been twice replenished, there was a rough supper, and oceans of punch and claret; the dancing stopped awhile, but someone ever kept up the music. Past midnight, past dancing, Harriet found herself lodged on a settee between St. Clair and Mary, who declared his dancing-pumps unsoled.

St. Clair leant, whisky-breathed, to shake Harriet's hand as one gentleman might another's. "Forgive me, I was too deep in my cups before to wish you happy."

"And you are a jealous bitch, St. Clair." Mary snorted.

"Maybe, but not a fool. I do, drunk as I am. Wish you happy." St. Clair blinked the careful blink of the foxed, and rubbed at her nut-brown hair so that it spiked. "I was not to have her, not after Waterloo; and you seem to have some sense. God knows you are beauty enough."

"O'the contrary, madam, I should say she was not Fleming's sort."

"…What?" Harriet was two sips of claret too deep for banter, and grit her teeth at the poor showing she made. "What on earth?"

"A wit would answer, you have not hooves and a tail." St. Clair trailed off a moment into tipsy harmony, slumped into Harriet, and then held herself, over-careful, to the arm of the settee. "Dear Mary thinks Fleming has overshot her mark, and ought to keep her eyes lower in the world."

"She is exceeding private, is our Fleming, even among the company. If we fancy a—ah, I'll spare ye, madam—if we fancy one another, it goes on all in the open. Fleming is too good for it." Mary seemed not the least perturbed to gossip so. "The captain—and the captain hath not overmuch blunt —keeps a room here, at Mother Hannaford's price. The better to beguile game girls in private!"

"Merrifield, you clapped-up cull, you know that is not so." St. Clair stabbed him with her nib. "She keeps a chamber, yes, but I never saw her lay a fingertip to a game girl; it is for our comfort, not the captain's."

"I am afraid I miss your import," said Harriet.

"She dreams," said St. Clair, with a sad twist of her smile.

THE ROOM at the top of Mrs. Hannaford's house was meant for an upstairs girl, or a minor footman; the bed dropped down from the wall, and scraped the door and the clothes-press. Someone had aired the pillows and turned the linen back; the piled quilts were old and ugly and clean. The washstand was hard against the fender, and the window slanted half into the ceiling, but there were two burning candles upon the chimney-piece, and the fire was made lively.

"Our accommodation, madam." Fleming bowed as far as she might, and let the latch fall behind them.

She knew, very suddenly, that Harriet tasted of claret punch; her touch along Eleanor's waistcoat was soft, searching.

"All right, Harry?"

"I am bored of you being everyone else's," she answered, one hand tucked under Nora's breeches front to worry the buttons. "And in your shirtsleeves all the while!"

"No one else's, upon my word."

"A gentleman," Harriet said, indistinct against Eleanor's shirt, "is never without his coat. And I mind how you sang to that St. Clair!"

Eleanor laughed. "That St. Clair, is it? She had one song of me; you had the other six."

"I don't care." Harriet ducked out of her shift, when

Eleanor raised it, unbalanced and landed all on one elbow upon the bed.

"You are not too wrecked to remark, I hope, that I danced only with you?"

"Not wrecked in the least," Harriet lied.

"God's sake, woman, why must you favor these drawer-things!"

"And you attempt to call me tipsy, Captain?" Harriet went headlong into giggles. "A cav'ryman who cannot handle the ribbons!" She rolled aside, gasping mirth into the pillows, until she knew Eleanor no longer touched her.

In the brightness of the room, too small by far for shadows, Eleanor stared at Harriet's naked back. The gown she had just unbuttoned fell off the bed to pool in the dust of the floor.

"Oh, these I have had from a child." Harriet looked over her shoulder, fingered what scars she could reach, and shrugged. "I gave when first I met you that Pater could not abide cleverness."

"I thought your father was an invalid."

"He had the arm gone, when I was above twelve or fourteen," Harriet agreed. "He had Alfred to do it, and there was no stinting."

"He gave his man to beat you, the—"

Harriet laughed. "I s'd give a sackful of guineas to see Alfred while you called him Pater's servant! He was my brother."

"Your brother!"

"Sherry is not an elder son. Surely he spoke—or perhaps not." Harriet eluded the press of Eleanor's hand, lay on her back and gazed up to the plaster. "I am foxed enough to be talking of this, madam; were I you, I should turn to a different advantage."

"Harry…"

"Enough, Nora. I am abed with you in a mad-house, in my skin. If you should rather talk over unpleasantness, I will see if Miss St. Clair is waking."

"Upon my word, you would fall down." Eleanor's kiss was half a smile. "And she knows nothing I don't know."

HARRIET WOKE WARM, with a quilt against her skin and midday sunlight lancing in her eye. She reached for Eleanor and curled forward, out of the brightness.

Her hand closed upon bed-linen. She sat up with a shock.

"Nora?" Hoarse with sleep, Harriet called to her, though from its silence the tiny room must be empty. The fire was banked, and water stood by, not cold yet; Eleanor's boots and her sabre on its strap were gone. She was quite alone, in the strangest house she had ever visited. No creak of floor or ceiling gave out the presence of women, men, or otherwise, and fiddle and pianoforte no longer sounded from below. Harriet might have passed the night in a fairy-ring, but the fair folk had left Castile soap and an empty chamber pot.

She would have given much for a brush and a handful of hairpins—hers were hopelessly gone in the bed, or in Nora's pocket—but Harriet managed to put her curls up decent presentably, and to fasten her smoke-smelling gown. She took her wraps and reticule, kept her slippers in her hand, and stole into the corridor.

No maids, no mollies, no footmen, waistcoated women, or ghosts watched Harriet down the staircase. All was still and quiet as any grave. When Harriet came to the downstairs withdrawing-room and found a fire, and coffee, and breakfast, she could scarce believe it real.

"You've come down late," said Mrs. Hannaford, from behind the chocolate-pot.

Harriet, inelegant, yelled.

The house's owner wore morning weeds and a white cap starched high as any dowager's. Set between her teeth was a pearl-stemmed pipe. "Give you good morning, Missis Fleming. Your captain is away to the steeplechase."

"With what money?" Harriet's reticule chimed with coin when she shook it.

"Oh, not to wager, duckling. To race. I believe she was spoiling for a ride." Mrs. Hannaford looked Harriet up and down, grinned around her pipe-stem, and went on. "Do sit to breakfast. She enjoined me most strictly to your care. She will be back," the matron said, when Harriet hesitated. "With a prize, I dare say. I will not bite you, dear dark duckling. I do not care for 'em so young."

Harriet sat, as if the chair's brocade were gilt with hellfire. She could not regard the sausages in their jackets without picturing the molly-men and blushing; she took a spoon of eggs instead, and undertook pushing them about her plate with a forkful of mushrooms.

"You are shocked at my house, are you not? Had you not heard of the *femmes déguisées?*"

"I—I did not know there were more of them."

"Oh, my, many, yes. Some even carry it off deliciously as our Fleming."

"You have known her long, then?" Harriet asked.

"I have never *known* her, dear lady, pray put those daggers away; she has to now conducted herself most tiresome chaste. But I have had her acquaintance upward of ten year. I know most of us in Town, toms and molls alike."

Harriet tried the word, against her teeth and silent. She took a cup of ale, to wet her lips; made attempt again, and failed.

"My dear?"

"Is a…is that what I am?"

"I don't know, to be sure. The captain has never brought a lady here before—or a woman at all. You are most welcome, most welcome."

CHAPTER 13

"Fleming! Deuce take you, *giddap*, Fleming!"

Eleanor groaned. Harriet, beside her upon the carpet, was quicker; she threw Eleanor's frock coat down from the sofa, stood up and just as quickly ducked again. Sherbourne was teetering on the front steps, peering round to the nearest window in the morning dark.

"Oh," Eleanor said. "*Oh.* What's o'clock?"

"Half six," Harriet answered. "Pray lace me, before Sherbourne rouses the street!"

"Sherbourne!" Mr. Galvani might have shaken Eleanor's hand. She fumbled Harriet's knots and crosses, tugging until there was enough cord to tie somewhat, and smoothing the worst creases from Harriet's shift before buttoning her up the back; she had gone on to stuff her own shirt into her breeches before she saw Harriet's buttons all hindside before.

The knocking had turned to thumps of Sherbourne's fist.

"Remind me, madam, to refrain from seducing you 'pon hearthrugs! " Harriet felt over the mess with one hand, threw her cloak over all, and kicked under the sofa for Eleanor's boots.

"One never gets callers when it happens in the dreadfuls," Eleanor countered, and went down the corridor still jumping and pulling at her heels. "Stay there! Stay there, I'll keep him in the passage."

Sherbourne and a cloud of stale snow filled the narrow entry. In taking off his hat he knocked over the umbrella-stand; he tripped over the bootjack and half subsumed Fleming in his cloak.

"Major!" Eleanor staggered.

"I am treading near to drunk," Sherbourne said, enunciating to a nicety. "Good, you're dressed. *Allons-y, mignon.*"

"Where, upon my word?"

"Newgate."

"God, Sherry, you know I can't watch such things."

"You want to come to this one," replied Sherbourne. He pushed past Eleanor and into the firelit parlour. "It's young Carver."

Harriet heard that last; she watched Eleanor's countenance slacken, and in Sherbourne's shadow she thought Nora's hand went to the wall.

She sat exceeding still, for her part, cloaked, gloved, reticule upon her lap, curls arranged with spit and coal-dust.

"Jesus, Harry, you're calling early. You're only promised, you needn't fix his breakfast. Don't *give* him breakfast, he'll only cast it up."

"Give you good morning, brother," she said, and rose, and kissed his stubbled cheek. "You are awake passing early."

"I am awake late," he told her. "I want Captain Fleming upon—upon a matter. Go home, Harry, won't you?"

"Without an escort!"

"Lord God, don't be intractable, sister."

"I shall not be intractable. I shall go with you."

"No!" Sherbourne and Fleming spoke together.

THERE WAS a throng from Debtor's Door to St. Sepulchre,

and near an hour still to wait. Harriet was braced between Sherbourne and Eleanor, nearer the scaffold than shifted well, and kept from the cold by Sherbourne's fur-lined cloak and Eleanor's arm hidden round her waist beneath it. Under their feet a layer of rotten ice was melting; day dawned and the crowd became a crush.

Eight nooses were strung to the whitewashed gibbet, swaying gently.

"Who is Carver? What has he done?"

"Uttered false banknotes," said Sherbourne.

"My drummer," said Eleanor.

"Had his leg blown off in his first action, poor devil," Sherbourne went on. "Shrapnel struck the drum. Never mind his leg, had to pull him out of his horse. Bloody boy was twelve, upon my word."

"Seventeen." Fleming's arm tightened round Harriet's waist.

"He was nigh me in that Christ-forsaken field tent," said Sherbourne, no longer answering Harriet. He gazed ahead, above the crowd, and fixed his eyes on the gibbet. "By God, Spaniel, have you not a flask?"

"Captain," Harriet remembered to say, though *Nora* was at her lips. "If he was wounded out, he surely had a pension? Why then—how then comes he here for uttering notes?"

"Took to the poppy," Sherbourne said. Fleming was silent. "If Carver did put his mark on the notes, he was not in his mind; it is as likely he is a dupe, and taking the fall."

"Taking the fall!"

"Hush, Harry."

"But he may be innocent!"

"He has put his mark to a confession," Sherbourne told her. "And he was only a 'listed man, and the Crown will not care. Captain Fleming! Have you swallowed your tongue?"

"He is not innocent," Eleanor said, slow. "He did not forge a note. He is in pain, and a boy—only a boy. I believe he could not do it himself."

Sherbourne put his heel down sharply, cracking ice. Fleming pressed her hand over her mouth.

"Then he is—"

"He is a criminal, and dying shriven, as criminals die." Sherbourne had never struck her, but Harriet flinched.

By now the crowd was beginning to surge and murmur. Seven of the eight sufferers had mounted the scaffold from the yard; Eleanor began to shift nervously back and to. Sherbourne scrutinized each stricken face as it vanished under the rope and the hood, more and more uncertain.

"Spaniel, d'ye think…"

The eighth man was slim and spare of height, as a cavalryman must be; the ordinary and the guard who bore his arms across their shoulders seemed not to feel his weight. He came up the scaffolding steps between them on one leg, his tattered breeches swinging over a broken wooden peg. His face was pale and from his look it seemed, to Harriet, that more than his leg had been mangled. His eyes were quite as blue as Fleming's, ancient, empty.

"God have mercy."

"Steady on, Spaniel. He shan't care in a moment."

"Hats off!"

Fleming stood to attention. At the last, when the spectators sucked in their breath, she pulled Harriet tight against her side.

Harriet saw only the black of Eleanor's frock-coat, but she felt the drop shudder every sinew of Eleanor's body. Against her ear her lover's heartbeat skipped and raced.

Sherbourne gave a terrible groan. "See to my sister, you Methodist fool. I mean to go get wrecked."

It was a long time before Eleanor stirred. When Harriet lifted her head, the ropes had all gone still, the trap yawned black and the crowd was moving; Sherbourne was nowhere in sight. "H-how is it with you, Nora?"

"Bear me company, I beg you," she replied. "I have an errand that will not wait."

FLEMING'S ERRAND took them to a narrow cookshop on Thrawl Street. She did not make a courtesy or pretend interest in the gray-edged pies; she kept Harriet's elbow most tightly, and had kept Harriet's pocket since they passed the Bishopsgate. If Harriet felt strange at finding herself so in Whitechapel twice in the week, she did not remark upon it.

"I am here to call upon Mrs. Carver," said the captain to the proprietress, "Mrs. Tom—Elizabeth Carver?"

"Upstairs," said the woman behind the counter. She said nothing else, for fear perhaps that the flies might find a way through the indifferent fence of her teeth. The stairs were narrow as the shop, looped and carpeted with dust as though no one had come below in a very long time. Harriet saw Eleanor's hand drop across for her sabre, then fall away. Faced with the silence, the closeness, and the vinegar-sulphur smell, Harriet chose to follow Fleming up the stairs.

No one had made a light in the slant-ceilinged upper room, though the day was clouded and cold, and it was not clean. It was bare. By the hearth there was a ragged bedroll, and a stove-in crate that might have been for kindling, if it had not had such a nest of scraps and rags piled in it. A handful of pegs in the plaster of the wall held a cloak, a night-rail and cap, and a bucket; that was all. The window was clean, its gaps stuffed full of grimy, raveled yarn. There was one chair; a woman was sitting in it.

Elizabeth Carver was older than her husband had been. Her eyes were red-rimmed, and her costume was all dyed cheaply black. She wore her glory of red-gold hair tightly drawn, but it had begun to fall where the black crape band had slipped. Her dress fit secondhand, and her bosom was the more ample for nursing a child; she did not cover her breast with her black woolen shawl when they came in. She pushed a handkerchief across her nose, when she saw them in the open doorway, and fixed on Eleanor an amber-green gaze most shocking familiar.

"You may turn around the way you came," said Carver's widow. "I want nothing to do with the saucy Seventh, and least of all you."

"Tom wrote me that you had been safely delivered," said Fleming. "I was most glad to hear it."

"Oh, stuff your gladness in a nine-pound gun!"

"He was exceeding proud in his son, madam."

"How nice of the opium-eating son of a—"

"Lib, I'm sorry it went hard with him."

"And you may address me Mrs. Carver, Captain!"

"Mrs. Carver, I will not intrude upon your grief. I came only upon business—to bring a token from the regiment." Eleanor set coins upon the windowsill; from the sound of their fall, but few. After a long moment she added something Harriet could see, nearly: round, heavy, silver, on a ribbon of crimson and blue. Mrs. Carver closed her hand over the lot.

"One pound eight and sixpence!" She laughed, waking the baby at her breast. "That is a rich gift, for a young man's leg, for his life! And they sent you to bring it me, you charmed bastard, you who came back perfect! I wish—I wish he came never back!"

Eleanor had frozen. She did not raise a hand or retreat when Mrs. Carver struck her, with a fist still full of coin; she did not look up when Harriet cried out. It was Harriet, pulling and dragging at Eleanor's shoulders, who got them down the stairs.

Something whipped past Harriet's cheek and fell on the shop floor: Eleanor's Waterloo medal. She stooped, and clasped it in her glove, and had to run, suddenly, to keep up with Fleming. Square-toed boot prints were wide in the dust.

"Nora," Harriet risked shouting after her. She did not think the broadsheets came to Flower and Dean Street. Eleanor stopped, half in the gutter, and when Harriet reached her, Eleanor's face was wet and bruising.

"Forgive me bringing you here," was all she said.

"Did you love her?" Harriet asked.

"Lib? No. I—knew the pleasure of her company, but rather less of it than many. She washed for the Seventh, in Spain. Until young Carver, I never knew her to entertain for love."

"I think she might have loved you—by the way she hates you."

"Why should she not hate me? The Seventh killed her husband. The Seventh has put her upon the parish."

"Not for a month, at least." Harriet played her fingers along Eleanor's arm as they walked. "It was well done, dearest, but you ought to have shaken Sherry's pocket before giving up your own."

"He was a man of my company."

"That does not excuse you from eating!"

"Leave it, Harry," Eleanor scowled as Harriet pressed coins into her glove.

"Write me a vowel for it," Harriet said, "And then tear it up; before next quarter-day everything mine will be yours." She stopped in the middle of the street and turned, trapping Eleanor against her skirts, blind to the fish-sellers and game girls stumbling round them. Carefully, she smoothed Eleanor's frock coat and fixed the medal in place, giving it a last rub with her fingertip before walking on.

"You ought not give this up so lightly," Harriet said. "Not when it cost you so dear."

CHAPTER 14

The house in Clarges Street was cold when they returned. Eleanor disappeared into the larder, and Harriet stirred the downstairs embers, but could only rouse them enough to light a candle by. Its light was small; she left another burning on the chimneypiece for Eleanor and started upstairs, where there was more certainty of coal.

At leisure, now, she studied the portraits upon the faded wall. They were all stiff, solemn men and women, fair as snow, in the mode of a hundred years before. Black gowns and white stocks were only here and there relieved by regimental colors.

The first landing was given over to one painting only, and it stopped Harriet cold. It was well-colored and richly lit, and even candlelight showed, in the bottom corner, *David fecit…*

A young woman in a directoire gown gazed out, careless as she held a plain straw bonnet on blue satin strings. She was suitably solemn for her costly portrait, her fair hair all drawn to long, careful curls, but her eyes—very blue—were impish, awake, inquiring. *Eleanor Charlotte Our Sunny, in the Fourteenth year of her Age, 1804,* Harriet traced the plate at the portrait's foot. This was Nora, then, before the heavy weight of war and wounds and secrets. The day's chill fled, somewhat, as Harriet regarded her. Someone, once on a time, had loved Nora; enough to wish such a portrait made, to call her *Sunny*.

It made Harriet hum a little as she laid a fresh fire in Eleanor's bedroom, more generous perhaps with coal and kindling than those articles' owner.

"Don't do that!"

"What, humming?" Harriet sat back on her heels.

"You are no servant," said Eleanor, harsh into the cold.

"Nor you, but you have countless times seen to my comfort." Harriet rose, dusted her hands, and put aside the tray Eleanor carried. "I'll lay the supper. Look to your face —it's swelled."

"I want no nursemaid, either!"

"A fight is what you want, then, but let us eat first! You've taken nothing all the day."

Eleanor looked lost when Harriet touched her elbow. "Have I…Have I said something?"

"You have," Harriet's answer came short. Then she saw Eleanor's countenance, milk-pale and muddled, and half pushed her into a chair. "Sit down, dearest."

"It is only—I thought I heard—I saw…" Eleanor shook her head and lapsed silent, eating the cold collation of bread and cheese and remarking nothing. The room was grown almost warm, but she hunched further into her coat.

There was a wineglass on the tray—for herself, Harriet supposed—and a demi of wine; Harriet filled the glass and put it in Eleanor's hand. "I wish you would take this. It has been a terrible day."

"Lord God, yes, to have lost so very many!" Eleanor drank the glass off in one.

"Nora?"

"Harry," Eleanor answered her, sane enough, but a moment later she was trembling. "It has all gone so very badly, Harry, my love. Carver—I shall have to write Carver's mother—he will end himself. The poor boy will end himself! I knew it from his face. And what can I do for him, when I am called to the field three hours hence, and my fate?"

Harriet cried out. "Nora! Pray look at me, dearest, only look at me."

Eleanor flinched. She might have cowered, but Harriet held to her arms.

"Your fate is right here, with me," said Harriet, soft, and softer still. "We are alive, and in London, and nothing you see will harm you. Nora, pray listen, none of it is real."

She rested a moment on Eleanor's knee and was not struck for it or thrown aside; Harriet ventured to brush a kiss upon Eleanor's cheek. "This is real. And this." She slipped her hand under Nora's waistcoat, to her shirt; broke the laces and loosed the binding linen, and laid her palm over Eleanor's heart.

SHERBOURNE TOOK the letter from Linton and, as Eleanor watched him, went as crimson as the wax of its seal. He half-staggered up from the card table, their game forgotten, and out of the drawing-room altogether.

"Sherry?"

"Concerns you, I'd lay a fiver," answered Sherbourne, without meeting the captain's eyes. "Her, too. Harry! Harry George! "

Eleanor had left Harriet to a stack of books and a bowl of pears, tucked away in her room on Sherbourne's third floor; now, at her brother's shout, she hazarded two and three stairs at a time, and Sherbourne was perspiring round his cravat.

"What on earth's the matter, man?"

"Run for your very life," Sherbourne said, and Eleanor could not wager how far he was in jest. He held the letter up to Harriet, who had frozen upon the stairs.

"Addressed t'you," she retorted, though he had said nothing; the letter's long fold was writ edge to edge with Sherbourne's names. "Open it. I can't bear to, Astley, please."

He was not long in reading. "Mother is in Town, and expects I will be at home this evening. She is—she has heard your banns."

"Fuck me seven ways from Sunday!"

"*Harry?*"

Sherbourne made a noise in his throat of agreement, but not surprise. "Wash your count'nance, Harry-girl, and see to your turnout." He came far enough up the staircase to kiss Harriet's cheek; then, with a hitch of his lame leg, he turned round to Fleming. "This was just Mother's cannonade; she'll breach the walls by supper. Go up with her and see to the defenses, will you?"

"THESE ARE ALL YOU HAVE?" Harriet frowned into Eleanor's traveling case. "I think you look well in them, but they will not pass before Mother." She said the name as Sherbourne did.

"Awfully heavy weather you make of this—both of you. I thought your mother in her dotage, painting watercolours by the sea-side."

"Mother is fifty-nine," replied Harriet. "And I beg you, dearest, do not mistake your measure of her. She is…" Harriet shook her head, sharply, so that she had to push curls back into her bandeau. "You do not mind your tailoring second-hand? Sherry was a beau, before he took so well to letting out his waistcoat. There must be half a dozen suits of evening dress upstairs."

"Evening dress! May I not put on my regimentals?"

"Not for Mother."

Rifling Sherbourne's cast-offs did not soothe her. Harriet sorted over shirts plain and ruffled, piled cravats by color, and mounded twenty coats upon the counterpane. None seemed to pass her muster, and each chime of the clock nearer supper-time brought fresh curses.

"If your mother troubles you so, we might take better care to avoid her."

"She is my mother, madam; what do you suggest?"

"I might post to India."

Harriet sent a pearl sateen waistcoat at Eleanor's head.

"Harry." Eleanor sat down upon the hassock Sherbourne kept to prop his leg. She tried twice to seat Harriet beside her, but she seemed in frantic flight between the hat-stand and the clothes press. At last Eleanor put out her boot, and caught Harriet when she tripped.

"Only tell me why you and Sherry dread this."

"My mother is coming! You look fallen from the rag-bag, and my mother is coming! Here!"

"I have asked for your hand, Harry, I must ask it *of* someone."

"She will hate you, Nora, for every reason I love you, and she will make it known, and make it hurt."

"If she hurts you, she must contend with me."

"You would deprive her of her greatest sport? Of all her girls, I am the disappointment; and worst, I lived!"

Eleanor kissed the crown of Harriet's head, to quiet her, but she went on speaking as if worrying a wound.

"When she learnt I was c-clever." It fell like a curse. "And when I had my season and came to naught, Mother consented I might squander awhile on books. She wrung Pater over it—oh, she must have—and he sent me out to seminary. It was a long way from home; I was fifteen years old. You, I think, were seventeen, and Sherry twenty? So you and he bled honorably for England, my sisters padded out the draggling fortune, and I was sent down in disgrace."

"Your marks were poorly?" Eleanor's brows told disbelief.

"Oh no. I am afraid it was my deportment." Harriet twisted free, and turned again to the silk and velvet storm blown across Sherbourne's bed. From its costly depths she pulled a sleeve, and then a coat, all of black velvet with black braid and facings.

"Am I to squire you to supper, or lead the Riderless Black?"

Harriet did not laugh. "Will it button?"

Eleanor, obliging, went to shirtsleeves; the coat was broad enough in back and shoulders, with caverns for arm-holes, but the hooks left her slip-fingered and swearing. "You would—ah! Bugger—you would leave the story there?"

"What story?"

"How you were sent down from seminary."

For the first time in an hour, Harriet fell still. Eleanor came to her, and went unnoticed.

"Harry...?"

"When I met you—when I met Nathaniel Fleming." Her

eyes closed tight. "When you kissed me I thought I should die of it and I thought—*thank God, I am no monster after all.*"

"You were a captain at Waterloo, and you are a captain still?" The dowager countess had a raven's eyes, keen and clever; she lacked Fleming's height by a full hand, but leant out from Sherbourne's chair as though she would overtop the captain even seated. It was the first she had spoken, having sat through her son's introductions and drawn sips of tea between her teeth. She had greeted him and Harriet silently, and Fleming not at all.

"I stood captain at Orthez," replied Eleanor, "under my lord Somerset, when Sherbourne was made Major. I was offered major when we posted to France, my lady, but I declined."

"You had rather stay a field officer than have a command? I much question it."

"I wished to remain in Sherbourne's command. A company is enough for me, and I find I turn my hand well to the horses."

"You are a groom, then," snapped the dowager countess. "It is a fine thing for a gentleman to admit!"

"Sherbourne is yet Major," said Eleanor quietly.

"Oh, my son has thrown away too many men to make general."

"My lady—"

"You need not defend him. One may read dispatches even if one is a female."

Across the room, Harriet had laid her hand upon Sherbourne's knee, and rested her forehead against his temple. It seemed they kept each other from flying to pieces. Fleming, with no one on whom to lean, crushed the carpet beneath her boot-heels and was careful not to pick up her teacup, lest it snap.

"It has been my great honor to serve under your son."

"You do not say overmuch with that. And I did not come up to Town from concern for my son. Let us come to it, Mr. Fleming. How much have you per annum?"

"Mamma!"

"Harriet Georgiana, if you have sold yourself without consulting me, I would know the price."

"I do not consider I have bought your daughter!"

"What do you consider marriage, then, Mr. Fleming?"

"My lady, I have the very good fortune of a love match. If it ease you to know, I have one hundred and twenty pounds from His Majesty, and some small percent of my own in the Funds."

"Very good fortune you may call it," said Countess Sherbourne. "When your bride brings near twice your income, and you will be shot of her the moment she is in childbed!"

Eleanor found herself on her feet, of a sudden, fighting the mad desire to strike the countess broad on the cheek. "I believe there is no one left in this room to bear insult, save the pianoforte and the clock; the one is not in tune and the other not in time. Pray go on, my lady, and belittle them. As to Lady Harriet's portion, you may keep it; we shall dine the more content without it, if only I must not bear you across my table of a Sunday."

"Sherbourne!" The countess drew back as though Fleming might bite. "Sherbourne, your captain!"

"At ease, Fleming," said Sherbourne, without rage or rancor. "Harry—Harry, darling, don't—ow! Deuce *take* it, Spaniel, get after her, before she ends in Fleet Ditch."

CHAPTER 15

*E*leanor waited to speak until the coach-springs had stopped creaking. When the cab door no longer quivered from slamming, Eleanor drew the hangings and latched it to.

"Where did you say we're going?" It was a moment before spots stopped dancing before her eyes. She was a muck of sweat under the close black-velvet coat, and all her anger had given over to the wish her tailoring might not kill her.

"Gretna Green!" Harriet cried aloud, eyes brighter every moment. She huddled in the corner of the carriage and glared back at Eleanor. "I had not thought, truly. We may as well go there, if you insist on bearing me company."

Eleanor took off her borrowed hat and Sherbourne's pearl-buttoned gloves, and rapped upon the roof. "Gretna Green, if you wish it," she said.

"Oh, do not tempt me!"

"Vauxhall," Eleanor shouted up to the driver. "Go by Regent Bridge, and breathe your horses. We've the time."

She kissed Harriet, who was willing enough, but passive; every jolt of the wheels separated them once again.

"Harry, dearest."

"Lord God," Harriet got out, her hands tensed and striking against her lap. "Lord God, she is worse every time! She behaved unspeakably to you, Nora!"

"Were I the dowager countess Such-and-So, I should not like my last daughter to marry a half-pay cavalry man."

"Sherry's captain, and a gentleman!"

Eleanor stroked Harriet's shoulders and spoke low, her words woven with hums and hushes as though she soothed a skittish horse. "She is not much in company, love, and it came unexpected—"

"Madam, you will stop. Defending. My mother."

"Harry, Harry. I was only trying—I fear you will go off like a gun."

"It is that woman. You see now why Sherry keeps her at a distance, why—*Nora!*"

She could not look up, nor make an apology, as Harriet's hands were pressing in her hair. Having gained all she could by stealth and speed, and thwarted only a little by the cut of Harriet's new bodice, Eleanor gave herself up for trapped. She drew Harriet's nipple against her teeth, sucking and biting by turns until white velveteen and linen were soaked through.

"We are…in public!" Harriet held her away. Her eyes were sparking still, but not with rage.

"We are absolutely not, madam, but at your word I will find something better to do."

"Yes—no—not that—not in a cab."

"As you like," said Eleanor, and pulled Harriet into her lap.

"You said you would stop!"

"Said I would find something better," Fleming corrected. With one hand she teased the breast she had neglected, until Harriet's rocking against her had nothing to do with the coach. Her other hand roved and sought at Harriet's hip. "Pocket?"

"Wh-what?" Harriet's head had gone down upon Eleanor's shoulder, and all her dark curls escaped their fillet.

"Where's your *pocket*," gasped Eleanor.

"N-no pocket-cuts in an evening dress!"

"Oh, fuck fashion." Eleanor cast Harriet's skirts up round them both.

"*Captain*," Harriet breathed. Then she was writhing against the slow circling of Eleanor's thumb, moans bitten back with each jog over the pavement. Someone had torn away Nora's cravat, it was all disarray, there was a carmine-mark at Nora's throat and it was just where Harriet's mouth fit, just so…

"All right, Harry?"

She half whined in frustration and fumbled for Eleanor's wrist. "Yes, please, God, please, *inside me.*"

"Servant, madam," Eleanor said, and shifted, so all Harriet's cries were lost in Eleanor's coat.

ELEANOR'S HAT HAD, somehow, gone quite under the carriage-seat; she was obliged to brush it back to respectability on the walk down Bridge Street. At the garden turnstiles, her pocket was heavier by a sovereign, and Harriet was very taken with straightening her gloves.

"I have not come here in years," Harriet said, tucking her forearm against the plush of Eleanor's coat. "Not since they gave the triumph for Wellesley, and Sherry came home on leave. What a pity I did not meet you then! Where were you?"

Eleanor raised her brows, as if she could not remember. "Vitoria? I believe I was horse-thieving off the Spaniards. I wore not stars enough to come home and stroll in gardens."

"Were you so handsome in regimentals then, stars or no?"

"One hears," said Eleanor, when Harriet answered her blushes with a smirk, "Mrs. Hengler's fireworks are a marvel."

"I have never seen them; Sherry does not care for rockets." Thousands of wax-lamps burned all round them, throwing silver upon every face that passed, but by the press of her arm Harriet led them down toward narrower, darker lanes.

"And you do not care for the lights?"

"I care chiefly to get *away*. To be no one's daughter, to do what every soul comes here to do."

"You are sure?" They had left the lamps all behind; ahead the darkness was held and twisted by untended trees. Voices carried to where they stood, from within, but the sounds were spare of words.

"Why, by God, must you be twice the gentleman of any man alive?"

"It is only—they have a reputation, the dark walks."

"Then you had better accompany me, and save my name," laughed Harriet, "As you dare do no worse than watch the rockets go up."

"Harry…"

"Oh, come, Captain Fleming. Boney is locked up at Longwood; come." Harriet entreated, both hands coaxing at Eleanor's velvet sleeves. "I give you my promise, nothing's to fear in the dark."

When first the fireworks whistled, Eleanor shivered; the sky above the trees' enclosing black bloomed red and blue, and her tremor carried down Harriet's arm.

"'s well," she said, through her teeth, when Harriet hushed her.

Harriet shifted and sent them off the path, out of the glare of falling embers. Eleanor, with Harriet's weight upon her, found her back pressed to the bole of an elm.

"At ease, Captain," said Harriet, so Eleanor must breathe at least enough to laugh. Even then she stood stiff in the stiff evening coat, and the slide of Harriet's glove over cheekbone and throat did not still Eleanor's shaking.

"I meant only to give you fair wages for your conduct in that cab," Harriet whispered.

"…But?"

"Stay with me. Nora." Harriet kissed her, once, slowly. She cast her gloves away and then, in the dark, she went to her knees.

Eleanor was not armed; her front fall was no matter, and

trousers of superfine had more pleasure to offer than riding nankeens. Harriet rested her hands a moment on Eleanor's hips. Through the fabric she could trace the pulse in Eleanor's thigh, and beneath her left thumb was the indent of a scar she did not know.

She leant and kissed it, to learn it the better, and Eleanor moaned.

At the first press of Harriet's fingers she forgot herself. She was half biting against her own hand, but no man in England sighed and breathed *please* like that. *More* and *harder* Harriet gave, when Eleanor asked it, and shifted to take Eleanor into her mouth.

"Harry, *oh God*," and all Eleanor's weight was braced down in her boots and at Harriet's left hand, and still with her left thumb Harry circled the unfamiliar scar. After some time she felt Eleanor's fingers drift from her hair; she stood, shook off leaves, and let Eleanor stroke where a bramble had scratched her cheek.

She plucked the handkerchief from Fleming's sleeve and patted her lips, as if she had been careless with an oyster. Then Harriet reached to gather back Eleanor's hair and was herself swept up, slippers clean off the ground, Nora's voice ragged beside her ear.

"To home," she begged, "And t'hell with anyone who sees."

"No. My rooms. My bed. Mine." Harriet insisted with kisses still salt-edged.

"And if thy mother should spy us?"

"With a man, this time! Why, she'd be dead of joy."

HARRIET'S BED in her brother's town house was not so warm as Eleanor's, nor broad enough for two, but they had gotten some use from it. Eleanor's head rested on Harriet's shoulder; her borrowed silk shirt and her stable-scarred hands were against Harriet's bare skin. Until Harriet reached for a new book, she was asleep.

"Be still, Captain, it is not your watch."

Unpossessed of words yet, Eleanor lifted a brow toward the fresh novel, the half-burnt candle.

"I do not sleep with Mother in the house."

Nora shivered awake, stretched, got half Harriet's hair under her elbow and dented her hand on the bedstead. "Wish you'd told me. You know I'd have sat with 'ee."

"I know." Harriet's kiss was more fondness than desire. "I have now had it from two persons that something troubles *your* sleep," she continued, light as air. "I fear I must mistrust them, and one my own brother! Madam, you lie like a stone."

"That is—not usual. The dreams," she said, and would have turned away, but there was nowhere to look but the hangings or the ceiling. Her breath began to choke in every pause. "For years, until you, and this—the most terrible dreams."

"What do you dream of?"

"Bayonets." She drew back from Harriet's touch, as far as she could without falling from the bed. Harriet took hold of Eleanor's shoulders, making stubbornness serve where her strength was less.

"It was dark, dead dark, but for the guns. My men were— we were cut to ribbons, we were *fucked*, and instead of *turn about*, it was *hard again*. Those bayonets, in that dark!"

"But you led them," said Harriet.

"I led them to die!"

"I have seen drill enough to comprehend that a captain is well-placed to die."

"You asked of my dreams," the captain said. "Ten times a night I refuse the honor of the charge."

"You'd have been shot."

"If our places were exchanged, and you knew by your own life you might spare eighty—*eighty*, what should you have done? Or are you too much a lady to call me coward?"

"If I thought you a coward, Captain, I do not suppose you would know my Christian name." Harriet withdrew her embrace. "Say you had deserted; ten minutes later some other fool would have taken the field with your men, and they should all be dead for want of your common sense."

Eleanor was so still that Harriet could touch the marks of sun and wind at the corner of her eye. She kissed lightly as breathing where her fingertips had brushed. "And my heart should have broken on the moment, I am sure of it."

CHAPTER 16

*F*leming came whistling into Sherbourne's breakfast-room. He was reading a sheet from Ackerman's with his boots upon the table and his chair keeled dangerously back; when he spied Eleanor there was a sudden series of thumps.

"Have you had your hair in *curl papers*, man?"

"We can't all have bonnie barley-curls like you, Sherry. I thought it proper to lay on the *comme il faut*, since you have invited the entire regiment this evening."

"Paget and Wellesley—his grace Wellington, besides, and the King's Own, and the Greys, and a deuced number of the Ninety-Fifth on account of Beauchamp," Sherbourne agreed. "Give you good morning. Have—have your eyes been like that always?"

"Blue?" Fleming laughed.

"Blue fiddlesticks. Sparkling, like."

"Sherry, have you been dipping into the punch?"

"If I have it is my punch, but upon my word, only coffee, and that while waiting for you. What kept you? Your lady wife, as will be, is away to your house in your absence, likely shoveling the lot on a bonfire."

"Threadneedle Street," said Fleming. She dipped into her waistcoat and tossed a blue velvet bag onto Sherbourne's bread plate.

"Christ Jesus, moonstones!"

"I was ever Grandmamma's favorite." Eleanor looked wry. "Do you think they will suit her? And do you mean to ask me to breakfast?"

"Suit Harriet? Spaniel, I thought you meant me to sell them and finance tonight's crush." Sherbourne waved at the covers upon the table. "*Ask* you to breakfast. You never *asked* for my fry-up at Spain, just stuck your miserable fingers in. Don't let it differ now you're to be my brother!" With a last look into the velvet bag, he returned it to Fleming and helped himself to bacon.

There was a letter propped against the coffeepot, *Captain Nathaniel Jas. Fleming 7th Queens Own,* in a hand Eleanor did not know, sealed with a pale-blue wafer.

"Oh," said Sherbourne. "You'll want to look at that."

Her pulse crept up to the back of her mouth, and her empty stomach knotted. She thought of discovery, of blackmail, of some 'listed man in Bournesea who had heard the banns and somehow—*how, by God?*—knew the secret. She cracked the wafer and closed her eyes.

It was a note on Sherbourne's bank for three hundred pounds.

"What's this?"

"Money, Fleming. Buys things."

"Sherry—"

"It is a wedding-present, damn you, and you'll draw it tomorrow. A woman's tack is a deuced expensive thing, and I guess she will want a new costume to be wed in. They're silk, generally. You might see to your own turnout—I believe you stole those gloves from a Spaniard at Badajoz. And for God's sake, you may wed in regimentals and a shako, but spare the honey-moon the sight of your grandfather's hat."

He went on, through the platter of buttered eggs, the ham, the coffee and sugar, and the apple-pie dish. "If there is any over, call it her allowance for the annum. I'll keep it up— and if she gets you an heir, I'll double it. But I hope, lad—" Sherbourne looked as if he had bitten a hornet in his egg-yolk. "I hope before God she does not. None of the girls out of Mother have shown up to breeding."

Sherbourne drove his spoon into his apple pie so that the plate clinked, making an end to the subject. "Any road, Fleming, we must drink to your last hours as a free man. It is only brandy; I promise not to get you foxed and spoil your curls."

HARRIET WAS BEAUTIFUL. Eleanor did not find it indulgent to think so, as that lady stood by in white mull shot through with silver tinsel; she had said *nonsense* to silks in seven colors, and made threat to cry in the middle of the modiste's, until she carried the day. She had spent almost more on the shoulder-gloves of snowy kid, the better, she said, to show up Fleming's white facings. Would they not stand all the evening arm in arm? The Moorlowe opals, in their old, old setting of silver, Harriet had sponged for an hour before letting Eleanor fasten them round her neck.

"They are your inheritance," Harriet had said. "It is a pity I cannot see you wear them."

Eleanor, a smudge of bootblack on her nose and her white sash open at the waist, had laughed at their reflection in Harriet's glass. "They do not suit with my dolman. But..." She had given her whispered promise to wear them, if Harry so wished it, as soon as night found them alone.

The memory warmed Harriet more than the three dozen candles Sherbourne had spent on the room. There was no trace of bootblack about Eleanor now; her turnout was flawless, bold white and blue, and her dress sword bore a better gloss than Viscount Colonel Beauchamp's. She looked, in the candlelight, younger than Harriet could ever have imagined her, and she was ever smiling when Harriet found her glance.

"My lord Captain, you look a dashing figure."

Eleanor bowed, smothering her grin behind her glove. "You will insist on calling me that?"

"I will, because you like it." Harriet rose out of her slippers to lay a kiss on Eleanor's cheek. "For my part, I mislike your dress boots make you so much taller. It pleases me to regard you eye to eye."

"I mislike the dress boots," Eleanor assured her.

"Thank you, for this," said Harriet, suddenly nervous. "For…for going on display. For my sake, for the party. It is a foolish fancy of Sherbourne's that I should want—"

"That you should want, for once, what your sisters had? That all the *ton* should look at Harriet Gresham and know she is not lacking?"

Harriet swallowed, and pressed Eleanor's hand. "I forgot you should understand," she admitted, low. "And I did not suppose you knew my surname."

"We are to be married."

"We are to be married," Harriet agreed. She could not help breaking into a smile herself.

"Oh," Fleming said. "Oh, damn." She struck at her chest, looked lost a moment, then gripped the fingers of her right glove in her teeth to pull her hand free. She fumbled at torturous angles beneath her pelisse and the stiff dress dolman as if a spider had dropped down her neck.

"Nora?"

"Moment," she replied, most anguished. With one last squirm Eleanor righted her uniform, rescued her glove, and showed upon the palm of her hand a small gold ring, crimson-set.

Harriet drew in her breath. "Oh—oh, Nora, I am too old for rubies!"

"You are not. You deserve them, if you will accept it."

"You are too generous."

"Not I. Sherbourne bought this. Against your happiness to come, as I remember, in case he should not be here to assure himself of it."

"He never waxed so sentimental 'pon my sisters!"

"Madam, I believe you may be something of his favorite."

Harriet came to herself with a laugh. The ring was bright and pretty and fitting, and she ventured it would fit. "I beg your pardon for all this speech of my brother. You perhaps have other things to say."

"Nothing you have not heard," answered Eleanor, "but for *accept it, please.*"

"MADAM." The speaker had pitched his voice low, as if he wished only Captain Fleming to hear him above the bright chatter of the room. No woman was by—only men of the regiment—but he followed this address with a hand on the captain's sleeve.

Eleanor turned as slowly and coolly as if he had set a knife-point to her back. The voice she had known, but the face was near ten years distant in her memory, and she had never seen it clean of other men's blood. His spectacles were over on one side, just as she remembered, and his long, fine fingers had moved to her wrist and held firm. His name, she was sure, had not been put to the evening's invitations; he was the Seventh's best surgeon, and he had left Sherbourne lame.

"Mr. Callander?" The captain's voice was startled, perhaps, at the touch of another man's hand, but very correct. "What is this?"

"Madam, I had the honor of your care at Orthez."

"The devil you did!" Eleanor shook herself free.

"You do not now remember."

"I do not give it credit," she retorted, finding her full height and addressing the Seventh's surgeon afresh. "What on earth do you mean, sir?"

"You were most grievous hurt in the charge. Took a ball in the shoulder—"

"By grace I do remember that, sir."

"—and went over your charger's ears and into the ditch. You were sent to the rear quite witless."

"So were a thousand."

"You, madam, I remarked. You were distressing young, and —h-handsome. And your valet would not allow that I undressed you."

"No doubt he thought it best, handsome as you found me." Eleanor watched him die, a little, and died for her part. On a moment she wished, most desperately, never to have said it; she knew now that Callander would strike first.

"I—gave myself to forget," Callander said. "Until my summons came to this—this outrage upon the Regiment. I have kept your secret this long time, Captain, but you must not go on with this. To so dishonor the Regiment—to make such attempts upon the sister of a peer—" the surgeon reached out, catching Eleanor in the chest. "I cannot let this be."

"Remove your hand, Callander, or I will call for powder and shot."

Something in her countenance froze him; he drew away, dropping his gaze. "M-madam, I assure you, I speak because I do not wish to see you hang. If this were to come out, you know all honor—all bravery—your name and all your deeds should be as nothing. Your suit cannot go forward. It must not."

"I will consider you have been drinking, James," said Fleming very slowly, hard as flint. "The Major stocks a cellar exceeding fine. I am not going to call out a man in his cups, because I will not see my fiancée's evening spoiled."

Callander's throat bobbed beneath his tight old-fashioned stock. "Good God," he whispered. "Good God. Does she know? Is she complicit? Madam, what have you done?"

Harriet, breathtaking and smiling and not fooled for a moment, appeared at Eleanor's side and stepped half between them. "Oh, Mr. Callander, how good of you to come! My lord Captain speaks most highly of you. Is not the Lord Uxbridge bearing up wonderfully well in spite of his leg? I thought I heard him inquire for you, not ten minutes since…"

She gave quite a pretty shake of her curls, so that the opal earrings shot color; she looked up at Fleming so besotted that Callander was obliged to bow and leave them be.

Harriet blinked off the vapid cast of her features, and leaned gently upon Eleanor's shoulder. "Breathe," she said. "Breathe, dearest. I thought you would kill him!"

"I fear I must, Harry."

"Nora, it isn't funny when you look so—"

"He knows, Harry. He knows everything, and has known, and will see us ruined."

"Lord God." Harriet paled. "Must you go after him, Nora? I should—I should not have come between you. I saw him touch you and I thought—"

"No, you had the right of it." Eleanor swallowed. "I cannot meet James Callander. He is an old man; his war was hard. If he spoke truth, he has held his peace these ten years."

"Nora—"

"We must hope he meant only to bluff me."

"Nora, *he's gone*. I fobbed him upon Paget, and there Paget be; Mr. Callander is gone right out of the room." She did not say it with relief at all.

"Gone out of the room? How can he?" They stood at the very top of the room, the better to be well-wished and courtesied. They might as well have stood guard upon the doors. Harriet let go Eleanor's arm and pointed, openly as she dared.

"There," she mouthed, toward a baize hanging between the book-cases. It swung a little still, as though someone had brushed it.

"What's there, dearest?" Eleanor willed her voice level. Every nerve sobbed panic and stole her breath.

"My lord the Earl of Sherbourne's study," Harriet answered, gone whiter than her gown.

CHAPTER 17

"Sherry, please," Eleanor whispered. Harriet saw her brother gaze Eleanor up and down and through.

"No," he said, as if he had thought of something and found it wanting. "If it is true—if it is true, the devil may take you, madam, but I'll not ruin you. You need not look so at me. But you'll cry off this God-poxed engagement—"

"Astley!"

"Shut *up*, Harry." He rounded on Harriet so quickly that Eleanor could only half stand between them. "Captain Fleming," he said; his voice had gone thick and grim. "Is a man of the regiment, but he is not the marrying kind. And should he persist with you, Harry, he and I will meet."

Eleanor was pale. She stood still as if faced, alone and on

foot, with a troop of cuirassiers. Beside her, Harriet dropped into a chair.

"Courage, dearest." She went on one knee to take up Harriet's hands, and kissed them; she did not think Sherbourne had a pistol primed about him.

He stood, indeed, rooted to the center of the carpet, and passed his hand over his face to drive back sweat. "Ten years you were my right hand in the field, Fleming. I saw you into the saddle at Waterloo with your arm bound in my spare shirt. I thought you the bravest man I knew. I bloody well wept to send you forward, and now you cast it in my teeth!"

"Sherry—"

"I gave my charge at Waterloo to a *woman!*"

It had not happened so cleanly as that. Eleanor held wildly to Harry's hands, shut tight her eyes, but could not wholly stay crouched by the wing chair on the floor of Sherbourne's study. She felt as stomach-sick as Sherbourne sounded; he excoriated her for her treachery, for her sex, for the shame of his sister, but as he flung words at her hunched back Eleanor had gone three hundred miles away.

Sherbourne, on a stretcher, leg broken under his poor Kestrel, already going half-mad as it fevered, giving over his good pair of pistols and keeping rough hold on both her hands. "Best take them up to the field, 'Thaniel, I'm deuced indisposed." She and Fraser, and MacHeath of the Greys, drew lots from Fraser's shako for left, right, and center; shook hands all round, and said the last, ancient prayer. In Hades, gentlemen, *and in the strange light of evening she took her men up the left, and never saw Fraser or Archie MacHeath again.*

"Will you not answer when I address you, you bloody-minded bitch!"

Her face was wet, her chest was burning, and she had nothing to say. She realized, somewhat, that she stood on her feet, that Sherbourne had taken her up by the arm and was shaking her, as one might shake a small and irritating dog. Harriet, close by her still, was weeping.

With careful force Eleanor put off Sherbourne's hand. She turned to Harriet and held her, without knowing who steadied whom.

"Madam, I will see you pilloried. Put in Bedlam. *Horsewhipped.*"

"Bear up, Harry, my love." Eleanor kissed her forehead. "Let go, now, before Sherbourne makes a scene. If you came to harm over this—"

Harriet spoke, for the first time in a quarter hour. Her voice was not broken. "I am bearing up, Nora. I am not the first soldier's wife to say farewell."

"WHERE IS HARRIET?" She did not give him good morning. After a week's dead silence Sherbourne's summons had come, along with his carriage, forty minutes earlier; Eleanor had gritted her teeth that he thought he might still order her this way and that, but found herself following orders just the same. Now his town house might have been an outpost on the moon, so cold and strange it felt, and from the crown of her head to the holes in her boots she ached not to be here alone.

"At Bournebrook, you fool, d'ye think I'd have her within a furlong of you?"

"Major, if you've done her ill——"

"Don't be an ass. She's well, if wailing."

"If not on her account, why on earth send for me?"

"You've a problem in my library." Sherbourne seemed to hesitate. "Be you armed?"

"Of course I'm armed! I thought you meant to kill me."

"Good Lord," groaned Sherbourne. "Wait. No pistols upon you? Choose a pair from yonder."

"Sherry, even now I would not meet you. I will not."

"Oh, that's very nice, I'm much relieved. I tell you, ma —*madam*, you've a bigger problem."

When she took the best brace of French pistols from

Sherbourne's cabinet, and he did not protest, Eleanor began to know fear. "What the devil, Major!"

"I think it is he," Sherbourne rejoined. "If that gentleman keeps a house in Yorkshire." When he passed her, the major clapped her upon the shoulder, as he might have before any sortie. Then he opened the library door.

"Captain Fleming, Sir Colquhoun."

Her brother Colquhoun was still the handsomest man Eleanor had ever seen. In profile, at the window, his fair hair gone all to white, he was half their father, but for the lines of a sneer; half an Apollo. He was still full seven inches taller than Eleanor. A newspaper was folded over his hands, but in the sunlight she could see its leaves trembling. Without turning to the doorway, he began to speak.

"I have lately seen our name in the papers, Nathaniel."

If Eleanor leant upon her memory, she could remember the college boy who sang as often as she, *blow, winds, blow, my bonny-o*, but in the years since she had seen him his voice had grown chill and void of music.

"I own it a cruel thing to thus hear news of you, after so long a time! Did you not think of your lady, before you cried off this engagement? What do you mean by it? Did she come to you under false colours?"

"Never, upon my word," said Eleanor, and stepped from behind Sherbourne.

The newspaper fell to the carpet. Sir Colquhoun's gape was hidden by his gloves, and he had gone sickening pale. "God Jesus. It is Nora."

She legged him somewhat of a bow.

"Nate is dead, then, and you——"

"He is dead," Eleanor answered. "I am heartily sorry for it. And I am heartily sorry I could not marry Lord Sherbourne's sister, but you may see, Colly, all that fault was mine."

"All that fault a thousand fold," her brother said, and spat. When Eleanor brought a hand to her cheek, Sir Colquhoun made to seize her arm. "How dared you, you freak, you foul unnatural thing! I will take her in hand at once, Major, upon my word. I will bring her home and see to her, I swear it!"

"Why on earth," said Sherbourne, exceeding calm and dry. "Were I you, Sir Colquhoun, I should do no such thing. She has had twelve—rising thirteen year to dishonor your name, and you have only seen the papers Sunday week."

"She is my sister—mine—to settle as I will!" He swung at Eleanor, badly, but she should have been laid on the carpet if she stood for the blow.

She had been too long a man: she ducked, landed two hard punches below his ribs, and shoved her brother out to killing-distance.

"Hold!" At that moment, Sherry's voice was all that stayed her. He stood close by, as if they were comrades still, as Eleanor realized her sabre was drawn. Sherbourne's firing piece was near to her eye—and set at her brother's heart.

"You will not do violence upon a woman in my house, Sir."

"You consider that a woman!"

"She has killed better men than you, at His Majesty's behest," warned Sherbourne. "I own she is your sister, but she is of my regiment, and not released from my command."

"Then you mean to bear this insult!" Sir Colquhoun's eyes stared wide. "Have you no regard for your own sister?"

"That matter lies between 'Th—between the captain and myself."

"I am not so beguiled by her as you, Major, and I will not brook dishonor."

"Who is dishonored, man, but a pair of spinsters? Leave it lie."

"I will not!"

"Do you intend to meet your own sister, then, for getting your name in the *Times*? Upon my word, that will be sporting! She will drop you like a mad dog in the street."

"It is you I intend to meet, Lord Sherbourne, as you have drawn arms upon me—"

"In my house!"

"And as you prevent me thus removing my property."

"Colly, don't!" Eleanor put up her sabre. "Brother, I beg you don't."

"Do you care so much for kinship, then?" Sir Colquhoun's face was not so handsome in his anger. Red burned to purple across his cheeks and nose, and his sneer, at rest no more, became a rictus. "That is brazen of you, sister, when you defiled our younger brother's gra—"

"Enough." Sherbourne did not modulate his voice for the walls and windows; he pitched it for battle, and Sir Colquhoun flinched. "You, Sir, may gather your surgeon and seconds and give your notice to my man Linton. I will meet you as you like, but I will not bear sight of you until that moment. You, stand as you are, Fleming; if you *cry*, deuce take it, I'll rip your entrails out."

Sherbourne stood aside from the library door, and did not need to help Sir Colquhoun through it. When he had gone, Eleanor and Sherbourne regarded one another in terrible silence.

"You cannot kill him," she begged. "He has no children. Moorlowe will go to the Crown."

"Kill him? I don't mean to blood him! I mean to shame him home to the West Riding."

"You need not do so much." Eleanor much wished to take Sherbourne by the arm. "He is like Father—he is a man for a grudge, not a fight—put him off for a fortnight, and in a week's time he will remove to Moorlowe. If you take up his challenge now, he is a shot so appalling bad I fear he will kill you."

"I must, Fleming. He would have struck you."

"Had I not struck him!"

"I must," repeated Sherbourne. "You are a lady."

ELEANOR REGARDED six fresh cornets on horseback, and the six cornets, uneasy, regarded the captain and the dogcart full of melons. Broken old pikes and stakes of odd heights—a man's shoulder, a mounted man's eye—had been driven into the training-ground, and a flyblown green melon was impaled upon each.

"This is not the worst I shall ask of you," she said. "We have blindfolds for that."

She must, someday, omit that jest. Into the silence, she drew her sabre and brandished it, showy, aloft.

"I care near nothing for how you handle your sword at home. This is His Majesty's sabre, light dragoons and hussars, which I believe you

believe you are; it is a bloody clumsy, nasty weapon. When first you use it in the field you will, upon my word, throw up."

The young officers, as one, snickered. They were between eighteen and one-and-twenty; they had come to France already conquerors, they had never been uncertain of the morning. It pricked Eleanor to seething.

"Cornet Doyle, if you do not heed me upon the field you will surely die; you had best make a habit. You have read the book, I trust? You may, when it please you, demonstrate the six cuts and six defenses?"

"Yes, Captain."

"Sacré veinard, va! You may go last, then."

"D-don't you mean first, Captain?"

"Said last," Eleanor replied. "Each man shall have a turn round the field, and as it is a clear day and smooth going, he who loses his seat shall muck out for his fellows in the morning. I much hope your beast is high stepping, Cornet Doyle, as you shall make your attempt in a melon salad." She turned Malabar toward the start of the course, and only at the last moment gave a smile. "Make a good showing—no missed cuts, and no man unseats—and I will muck out for all of you."

Six grown lads stared as though the captain were Christmas dinner astride a horse.

She gave Malabar a touch with her heel and was away, sabre up to guard. The drill was part of her sinews, the timekeeping calls one with the pulse in her chest; she had to remind herself to shout for the cornets' benefit. Cut first, cut second, cut third, cut fourth, very grievous wounded melons slid in slices from their pikes; cut fifth, a bisected fruit spun off into the air.

Eleanor straightened and dipped into the sixth cut, the forecut meant to cleave a man's head ear to ear, and agony rolled from her wrist to her elbow along her scar. She dug into the stirrups and cried out.

There was a sharp crack, and Malabar shied, but not quickly enough to spare Eleanor a gouting spray of melon-juice. Soft shrapnel pattered over her shoulders, and where she had missed her cut there was only empty air.

"No misses for the captain, then," said a voice from stirrup level, some paces away. All the cornets' horses were prancing in fear.

Sherbourne, leaning somewhat on a brass-topped stick, holstered his discharged pistol and gave her a grin. "Observe you the captain is covered in guts, but none be his own. Protect each other; know each where the other is weak. And read the bloody book," he finished, coming despite his limp across the melon-sloshing ground. He took Malabar's head and led the horse to the edge of the drilling ground, while Eleanor bit her lip bloody. Then he handed Fleming down as he might a gently-bred lady, both the captain's hands upon his shoulders, though it wallowed him in sticky yellow as much as Fleming.

"I gave you took that arm from the sling too soon."

"I gave you are too much upon that leg," she said, low, not to contradict the major in front of the men. Aloud, Eleanor put a brave face to it. "Wasting powder and shot upon a canary-melon! It would have bled out, betimes!"

"Nonsense; you were a dead man."

That was too much like history; both fell silent, shoulder by shoulder. Major Sherbourne dismissed the men, and ordered Captain Fleming's troop horse bathed to a nicety, and Eleanor hunched at the waist and made effort not to faint.

"They'll never go in proper fear of me now!"

"Spaniel, your braw gold head shines in their nightmares."

"Wh-what brings you so far from quarters? You really ought not to be——"

"Deuce take the leg, dear Mamma," snapped Sherbourne. "I want your —your—advice."

"Mine!"

"It is—I mean to say, there is a personage…"

"A woman, Sherry!" Eleanor straightened up, fixing his eye.

"A woman!"

"Had your cherries plucked at last, then?"

He rounded upon her, but ended flailing, clinging to his stick. "Nothing like that yet," Sherbourne at last admitted. "Nothing so breathtaking. You must see her, Spaniel! And tell me what to do. I cannot break 'em to saddle by a look, like you."

Sɪʀ Cᴏʟǫᴜʜᴏᴜɴ Fʟᴇᴍɪɴɢ was making row enough in St. James' Park to stir the sleeping pigeons. He was so near a fit of apoplexy that Mr. Callander and Mr. Giles, the two surgeons appointed for the meeting, doubted the business could go forward at all.

"I refuse to meet you if the—if that person is your second!"

Sherbourne's captain, yawning behind a pearl-gray glove, seemed deaf and dumb. The captain held the major's pistol case and chronometer, erect as any footman despite the hour, and paid no mind to Sir Colquhoun's fine and escalating temper.

"I tell you I will not have that soldier here!"

"On what grounds do you object?"

Colquhoun would not bury himself so before witnesses, but Eleanor's heart stayed high in her throat. "Consanguinity, sir!"

"I should be fortunate in calling the captain my brother, or my son, but he is too fair for one and too ancient for the other! I have met your demand," Sherbourne said, his countenance all boredom. "Exchange with me, or go home."

The solicitor looked hard at Eleanor, but did not seem to unmask her. He came forward when she did, and shook hands, making his strides match hers as they counted off twenty. Eleanor had checked Sherbourne's flint and steel four times in the cab; now came the silly show of checking all again, priming and half-cocking, for the surgeons' benefit.

"You see what this has come to!"

"Do you shut up, Callander, or my womanish hand is apt to shake." Eleanor scowled down the barrel of one pistol, then its mate. "Dishonor the Major by a word and I'll meet you before breakfast. I have nothing now to lose." She holstered one of the weapons for herself, and gave the better balanced to Sherbourne.

"You are loaded, Major."

"I thank you, Captain." Without another glance, Sherbourne paced out to his handkerchief.

It was a clear day, and the mist was only very low upon the ground; Eleanor could see every line of him in his expensive tailoring, and wondered what it cost Sherbourne not to limp. She looked to Colquhoun's side of the field only once, as he took his pistol and brought it to guard. He was tall, yes, well-dressed and coolly mute in all his features, but so diminished Eleanor thought she must have shocked him near his grave.

Her eyes were not quite sharp, on a moment; she nearly missed the solicitor's hailing glove.

"Stand firm!" Eleanor lifted her own right hand in answer.

"And fire!"

Sherbourne's shot was more danger to the atmosphere, as Eleanor might have ventured; Colquhoun's went over-wide and blew a hail of bark. She shouted across to her brother's second.

"Are you satisfied?"

"The Major has deloped," announced Colquhoun's solicitor.

"The Major had rather not play at silly buggers," Eleanor snapped, not keeping now from the center of the field. "Will you not act in Sir Colquhoun's interest and take him home?"

"The contest must continue," Colquhoun's man said at last, as if he feared somewhat to do so while the captain was in range.

"We should not even be here, you—" Eleanor scored the turf with her boot, but said no ungentlemanly thing. "As you must, then."

Sherbourne gave a grimace when she came to reload for him. "Wouldn't let it rest, then?"

"No! God pox him, Sherry. Colquhoun has given that little lawyer he may not cede the fight."

"He is a little, round, unlikely thing, for a man's second. His legs are near to short as yours, Spaniel." Sherbourne watched the bullet down the muzzle, gaze as quick as Fleming's fingers. "I suppose I shall have to do Sir Brother some small hurt, before the light is up and the Runners come. Sorry for it."

Eleanor shrugged. "You are loaded, Major."

"I bloody well saw you do it! Haven't you more to say?"

"Be careful," she answered, and met his hand in the middle of the pistol barrel.

It was hers, this time, to call for the shot that might kill one or the other of her closest kin. It was four years since her last action, but Eleanor's voice had only one timbre for *Fire!* The sparks went up on both sides amidst a storm of startled pigeons.

Sherbourne's dark form never wavered in the smoke; Colquhoun was down, neatly, suddenly dropping from Eleanor's view. She forgot the *code duello* and broke for her brother's side at a run.

He was bleeding buckets—they must share stock, after all—but even with the surgeon wittering about, Eleanor could see the wound was no more than a tidy-edged gash at Colquhoun's right elbow. She went to her knees upon the turf, to sort what needed sorting. *See to it, Nora.*

"Keep her from me, Mr. Giles!"

No females in view, the surgeon gave way to the captain.

"Will you not let me die in peace!" Sir Colquhoun lay like an eel in the grass, making attempt to writhe from Eleanor's reach.

"You will not die today, sir." Eleanor knelt with all her weight upon Colquhoun's arm, winding and packing linen faster than the surgeon could hand it. "It is a flesh wound, and half what it might be. Go back to Moorlowe," she said, in the iron voice that sent her company forward. "Forget I exist."

Colquhoun had lost his wit, or else pretended senseless. He spoke to her not again.

It was some minutes later that she remembered Sherbourne's pistol. Eleanor unholstered and examined it for blood and damp, found all pristine, and looked about for its owner.

He leant upon a tree near her, his game leg tucked back, but came a few wincing steps to meet her. Sherbourne gestured out at her bloodied coat and breeches, and his own pain fled his face. He looked aghast.

"You're hit, Fleming!"

She shook her head. "Sherry, I was not in the fight."

"Oh." Sherbourne shook his head. "None yours, then?" He took the pistol-butt when she offered it, and holstered it on the second attempt. "And he shan't be so ridiculous as to die?"

"No, Major."

"Sure you're not hurt? Show the sword-arm."

Eleanor shrugged from her coat sleeve, obedient by habit; no blood was on the linen beneath.

"Thank God. I thought the imbecile had winged you."

"Not I," she said, parched suddenly of speech. She had known him half her life, and never seen the expression that darkened Sherbourne's features. He looked as if he had fallen from saddle at speed, and got upright again with no outward hurt, but every bone inside him had broken to filaments.

"We are…we are at quits, then, are we not? I suppose we must be. Wh-what a devilish thing." Sherbourne blinked at her. "I have had years to settle with—with burying such bits of you as Boney sent back upon your shield."

"Likewise you."

"This is different," he said, and she gave him the grace of turning on her heel.

CHAPTER 18

*I*t was not a bad trade, exercising horses of a morning in Rotten Row; the beasts were fine, the work was light, and she was used to the smell of stables in the rain. Eleanor had enough, with her quarter's half-pay packet, for coal and candles and letter-paper, and to pay for any letters that might come.

There had been two from Harry, at intervals of near a month—posted by the upstairs maid, Eleanor thought, on her half-holiday to Bournesea—and Eleanor had memorized them, Harriet's plain hand filling pages and margins with hope and sweetness and grief.

There had been one from Sherbourne, early on, to say that Capt. Fleming's dispatches of the 3d., 4th, 5th, 6th of the month &c. had been burnt unopened. Eleanor had cut the clean half from Sherbourne's sheet and thrown the words away.

The wind and rain drove her into a coffeehouse on her walk home; she sat dripping dry until just past nine in the morning, when she could no longer bear the smoke or the coffee, and consigned her dinner money to a cab.

A man in livery stood on the steps of the Clarges Street house, gazing like a mule at the knockerless door; he was stamping and hunching against the rain, and at Eleanor's step he turned to look fury out at the street.

"Captain Nathaniel Fleming?"

"Who wants him?"

"The right honorable the Earl of Sherbourne, sir, and he will 'wait your answer."

"How should you know I'm Fleming?"

"His lordship bade me look out a slight man and fair, sir— and you've come to the door with the key in your hand."

Eleanor came up the steps still tucking away the very small change from the cab. "Why the devil didn't you knock, man?"

"Knocker's not out, sir."

She mimed striking the cracked panels with her glove directly, rolled her eyes, and shouldered the door when it stuck. "Drip anywhere you like," Eleanor told the footman, "but I'm afraid my answer to the right honorable the Earl will be *go to hell.*"

The footman had taken out a slim letter, kept dry against his person. "He did say you would tell me to fu—fornicate myself, sir, but he said to tell you most particularly that it concerned your lady wife."

"My lady wife," echoed Eleanor. Her knees went loose and sent her to the floor. When she collected herself, she saw that the letter was a sheet torn from Sherbourne's diary, foxed all over the back with sums and scribbles. She took it before the tremor could reach her hand.

It was short.

Come at once. Sent enough change horses every post. Sherbourne.

He had sealed it without taking the ring from his finger, and he had sent his pocket. It was brimful when the footman handed it over, more than Eleanor had ever seen in ready money. She closed it and hung it round her neck, and started away for her greatcoat and pistols.

"Captain? Captain, what of your answer?"

"I'll carry it myself."

SHE HAD WINDED four horses before she reached the Essex

road, and now something was in it. In the setting sunlight Eleanor discerned six or seven soldiers, and two of their beasts, watching along a fence that stopped the road, sealed the ditch upon either side, and trailed away, sharp-topped and shoulder-high, into the fields. It had been thrown up in haste—she could smell fresh resin oozing from the stakes fifty lengths along—but it would be murder to try and get over. She shielded her eyes and picked out the bright white and brighter red of the Sixth Inniskilling, muskets and lances and all.

"Oh fuck, Harry," said Eleanor aloud. She knew no one in the regiment to bribe or to bluff. *Infamous,* Wellesley had called them, and not only for the way they hacked in the field; they made excellent riot-troops from their love of a riot, and even now they might be spoiling for a fight, sitting on post with nothing to do but scan the road.

She sat forward and rode straight on, because there was nothing for it.

"Stand who goes there!"

They waited longer to challenge Eleanor than she liked; it pricked her nerves to come so close to armed men on a strange mount. She paid too little heed to her hands—she was surpassing weary—and the hired stallion chafed and danced beneath her.

"Stand, in the King's name!"

"Evening, gents," said Eleanor. Holding the horse to rest, she pushed the handkerchief from her mouth and nose, the better not to be shot for a highwayman. Her voice was dust all the same. "What's all this? I did not know the Skins were on home service. "

"You have the advantage of us, sir," said the lieutenant who had been straddling the gate. "I am Lieutenant Oates of the Sixth Inniskilling, and pray who are you?"

"Captain 'Thaniel Fleming, Seventh Queen's Own, and pray give me the road."

The lieutenant regarded Fleming, hatless, gloveless, and grimed as she was, with a cavalry sabre to keep her greatcoat down and a pistol each side of her waist. He shook his head somewhat and then saluted her, as she had thought never to see again, but he did not open the gate. "Beg pardon, sir, but I cannot. We are put here to enforce quarantine."

"Upon my word I'll not prevent you. I will not leave Bournebrook while you and your men are posted here, and I mean to ride straight on through Bournesea village; but I must, I must away."

"Thirty souls have died in the village yonder; it's *sauve qui peut*, you're mad to go forward. Sir."

"I am on the Earl's business; I am ordered." She held up Sherry's letter with its blobby seal, though at a distance it might have been anyone's.

"He had hope of you yesterevening, before the guard was set," said the lieutenant of the Inniskilling. "Hard luck on you coming now. Last orders we had came from the lord Beauchamp, and they say *none to pass.*"

"It won't do," she answered. "I must to Bournebrook tonight, and my horse is near blown."

"We are obliged to fire upon anyone who tries to gain the road, Captain. Even a superior officer."

"Even Prinny," one added.

"It would take a deal of shot to drop Prinny," Eleanor said agreeably. "Well. I understand. Give you good night, sirs." She hunched her shoulders and turned the black horse's head, patting along his neck and sparing him every breath she could. "Oh, I am sorry, dear boy, I am sorry!"

She had never given a horse the spur in peace-time. Eleanor winced to feel the beast start beneath her; then it was all she could do to bring him back round to the gate and rein, hard and reckless, for the jump.

She saw the lieutenant and two others go aside; she shut her teeth and prayed none would go under. Next moment she was thrown up from her tack, legs and back and shoulders so punished she closed her eyes for pain.

The stallion was landing: one beats, two beats, three, *God do not stop*! Four and away, without a stop, without her neck broken on the stones. Eleanor came down into her seat and wept. She was away, and fast.

Shouts went up behind her, but they sent no rider, or else none would come into the quarantine. If the dragoons kept their word and opened fire, she never knew; let them try, limp over the horse's neck as she was, to take a bead on her head. She knew only that the ground was rising, the road rolling up toward the great house on the cliff. Eleanor pressed the horse up to hellfire; she would have taken stripes from one of her own men who did so, in battle, but it was not her own life she rode for.

"NORA." Harriet's voice had some strength left, though all her color came from fever. She held up her hands to Eleanor, and smiled.

"Harry." Eleanor smiled back, to steady her countenance. "How is it with you, dearest?"

"I am very low, I think, but not fever-mad yet. Or perhaps I am, as you have been here a hundred times since I've been ill, and held my hands then too."

Eleanor kissed Harriet's forehead. "Quite real, upon my word."

"Then you ought not to be here! Sherry's surgeon—so

dreadful, he *will* converse while he bleeds one—says it is some contagion from the village. I believe he pressed Sherry for a quarantine."

"The village is shut," agreed Eleanor. She perched close on the corner of the mattress, bracing Harriet when she would have flinched away. "By grace I don't take fevers—I had them all out as a child—so I think I may safely stay. Callander is a saw-bones, dearest, he's not your man for a fever. Whatever he's conversed upon, you may forget it."

Faltering a bit as she tried to reason it, Harriet frowned, "If the Bournesea road is shut, how came you here?"

"Rode," shrugged Eleanor. She pressed Harriet's scorching hands and stood, briskly, though all her muscles screamed. She took a sharp breath and cast back Harriet's blankets. "Cold," she warned, and then Eleanor came over faint.

She mastered it quickly enough, eyes lowered and palms unshaking against Harriet's bare legs. From Harriet's ankles up to the edge of her nightshift, crumpled about her thighs, ran a hundred thousand specks of brightest red, rough under Eleanor's hands like sand upon a letter.

"Nora," Harriet implored. "Nora, what?"

Eleanor tucked the sweat-sour covers round her again, because she was shivering hard; she sat again on the bed's edge and drew Harriet against her, letting Harriet cool her face against the buttons of her coat.

"You looked so frightened," Harriet said, muffled.

"An officer of the king's army, frightened!" Eleanor lied, brushing a kiss to the top of Harriet's head. "It is only miliary fever. Nothing that will take you from us."

"But Sherry sent for you." Harriet's fingers tightened along Eleanor's arm. "I know he did. He must think—"

"He thinks me prettier than Callander, I don't doubt. Or else he thought it should please you to see me."

Harriet laughed, hoarse, not a little strange. "Give over, Nora. He sent for you that he might not have me upon his conscience."

"I believe he sent for me because he knew I would not have you upon mine."

"Only promise not to bleed me again, dearest, and I'll absolve you." Harriet trailed off into laughter again.

"Fools bleed a fever," scoffed Eleanor.

"Huzzah," said Harriet, throwing her arms round Eleanor's waist. "I should never love a fool."

"FLEMING!"

Eleanor came to her feet on the moment, but could not find the will to brace for a blow. She laid her hand against

Harriet's lips, to make certain she breathed, and then might have staggered a bit, bone-weary and wrung with grief. "For God's sake, call me out when it is all over. Have me flogged or shot as you must, only keep out of it while she lives."

"Nathaniel—madam—bloody hell. How does she?"

"Out of her head." The ribbon had long fallen from Eleanor's queue; she forced the tangle behind her ears and ignored Sherbourne's regard of it. "It may be a mercy it's so."

Sherbourne had kept distance; now he came into the sickroom with his hands out like a beggar. "I swear if she is made well you will have anything you like. Anything."

"Sherry," she made bold to address him. "Have you slept?"

"Please," he said. "The best horse in my lines. Fifty thousand—a hundred thousand pounds."

"Pipe down, man. She is poorly enough without you raving. And you haven't got fifty thousand pounds."

"I swear it, Spaniel, bring her through this as you did me, and I will go on my knees to Doctor's Commons for your marriage-license."

Eleanor stared. Then she laughed, much as Harriet had; a sound at home in a death-room.

"Madam!"

"Perhaps not on your knees," she said at last. She touched Sherbourne's forearm, and he did not flinch. "I will do everything—everything, old friend, but God knows what will come."

"God save you, madam."

"Sherbourne, if you bow, I will break in all your teeth! The keys to your stillroom I will take," said Eleanor, when he looked blank at her. "And your ice-house."

CHAPTER 19

Sherbourne was close by her elbow before Eleanor heard his footfalls. She was stretched past weariness, aching in her last sinew, her eyes smarting as if spirits of wine had been dashed in them. Every murmur from the depths of Harriet's fever made Eleanor's heart a drum.

"Fleming," Sherbourne said. She was used to his summons, in all watches and all weathers; she sat up now, a little, and attended. The major held something, small, black—Eleanor might swear it was a Testament—in his left hand, and a leaf of paper in his right.

"Nora." Sherbourne had not used her Christian name since learning it. It sounded, now, at odds with his voice. "Nora, my dear."

Sense, breeding, education fled away. She gawped.

"I must tell you—your brother," he tried, who had written a thousand letters mourning a thousand English sons. "I came to—your brother—Moorlowe house in Yorkshire has passed to Nathaniel Fleming, a captain of my regiment, and I have here a letter inquiring that gentleman's direction."

Eleanor was still breathing, because she breathed like a landed fish. She thought she had got a nosebleed; something salt streamed down into her mouth. Sherbourne was white and unsettled when she regarded him, his hands sketching in the air as if he did not know what to bid them do. Eleanor reached and caught them, and it was nothing like taking Harriet's hands, but he held on fast as life.

"Stand down, Captain Fleming. I'll take this watch."

"Harry…"

Sherbourne helped Eleanor to her feet. "Eat. Sleep. Orders."

"WAKE UP, Major Queernabs, I have need of you." Fleming tapped Sherbourne with one of the empty buckets she had brought from the scullery. When he stirred only as if to brush off a fly, she laid the bucket on again with a thump.

"Give over! Christ, I've a head." Then Sherbourne knew his

surroundings; he sat up so quickly as to knock his tumbler into a pigeon pie. "Fleming. Harry?"

"I've laid on as much boneset as I dare, and poultice of yarrow to draw the fever from her heart; gave her to drink, and now your house has no water, Major, so we are going to fetch some."

"We," gurgled Sherbourne. "Staff for that. Don't be foolish."

"I have sent your staff to the lodge, before they are all taken scarlet. Rations to the kitchen-garden gate, mornings. Cellar locked, I'm afraid."

"God damn you," said Sherbourne, very slowly, holding to his head as if it echoed.

He spoke again only in the sunlight of the courtyard, having soaked himself under the pump until his curls were sodden down. "I wonder you are still standing."

"I must," Eleanor said, astonished. She bent to lay her buckets under the water, betraying the sleepless nights only by stiffness.

"What is it like to do everything in, in, what used you to say—"

"*In such weight, measure and number, even so perfectly as God made the world?*" Eleanor finished. "My lord Sherbourne, I had never a choice."

He hefted the full buckets away for her, replaced them with empty, and stooped to secure the yokes. It was something to do, besides gaze upon her weariness.

"A great house, and no servants in it to speak of; this command, I was bred to," Eleanor said wryly. She leant on the pump, stuck her head full beneath the water, and scrubbed at her face. Her shirtlaces had fallen wide, and she had not bothered binding through her long vigil by Harriet's bed; when she came upright, sputtering and blowing, she was obliged to cuff Sherbourne's cheek.

"Beg pardon," said Sherbourne. "I was only... only thinking..."

"Pray don't, or I will knock you into the trough."

He shouldered his yoke of full buckets, swaying only a little. "I thought, what a wife you would have made. You may see me into the trough now, Captain, if you like."

"I should have to fill the buckets again."

Sherbourne laughed, an echo of his laugh before Genappe had slowed his gait, before pain and drink had paled him. He squinted a bit, to regard her, and spared a hand from the chains to knock wet hair from his brow. "I—I must beg your pardon. Many things—"

Curtailed by the yoke, Eleanor tossed her head, as Malabar might.

"Your bloody brother, for one—"

"I do not blame you for Colquhoun."

"Beg you let me finish," Sherbourne got out. He followed her in slow step, with great care not to swing buckets into her knees. "My—Harry is—I should not have parted you."

Eleanor was silent, lip drawn between her teeth, from emotion or exertion.

"You are my great friend, damn you, damn the whole business! What was I meant to have done?"

"...Major?"

"It put me deuced out of countenance, that you were hermaphrodite, that my *sister*—but by God, it pricked me to blazes that there should be something about you I did not know."

THE STILLROOM WAS COLD, but Eleanor worked in rolled shirt-sleeves, folded near in half over the barrel of thieves'-vinegar. No one had fed or decanted it in Sherbourne's memory, and the barrel was near its dregs, but what remained—she had given herself a penknife-cut to test the acid, and cursed the walls blue for five minutes after—was screaming potent. She went on cramming rosemary, thyme, sage and lavender under the liquid that was left, beating and breaking the stalks with all her weight leant into her hands, until she was almost drunk upon the smell. She thought of her grandmother, Lady Linley, to her last year as every year, filling the barrel at Moorlowe and pouring a dram for the four thieves.

Lady Linley's black still bag, with its precious bottles all nestled in cotton, was in Eleanor's campaign chest, and Eleanor's campaign chest was in London.

"Bring it here, or I shall see you put to burial detail!"

The cornet had his head bound about with bandages stained red, but he saluted her and ran. He was Fraser's, she thought, poor Jack Fraser's, but in her pain the young man's name had left her. The air was close and hot and pungent with blood and bile, and a miserable rain was seeping through the tent.

Eleanor stumbled, swayed, and must have lost her senses. The cornet was pummeling her shoulder, and she was cast forward over Sherbourne's stretcher. The boy—Blakeleigh? Blackney?—held out the black kit bag, gingerly as he might a grenade.

"Help," ordered Eleanor, near shivering with pain. The sling was loosening round her right arm, cutting at her neck, and she had not much time to get this right. With her left sleeve she blotted sweat out of her eyes, but the bottles' neat lettering still swam.

"Be you lettered? The bottles are labeled, all. Hand me—ohh, Almighty—hand me Pyrethrum, and Comfrey-Calendula, and Four Thieves."

She took them in her left hand and stared, like an idiot.

"Captain?"

"Put this in his flask—all of it—and see he drinks; he shan't want to." Eleanor handed over the feverfew powder, wincing as one bottle chinked against another. "Let that busy him while I see to the leg."

"His leg, Captain! Master Callander has already set it."

"Does it strike you I could set a man's leg with one hand? It is the wound I care for, and it has lain too long in its dirt."

"Course the wound has dirt! He fell in the dirt."

And the dead weight of Sherbourne's horse had driven it deep; and the boneset's hands had touched a hundred dying men. When Eleanor uncovered the major's leg, the streaks had come, as she had known they must.

"Steady on," she said to Sherbourne, and emptied the bottle marked Four Thieves over his wound. He screamed, screamed until she shied her face in her coat.

"I am sorry, my dear, my dear, my dear." Eleanor went at the wound with her left hand wadded in new linen, until nothing black or green or yellow flowed. She packed the rough-edged gash with comfrey and calendula-flower, broken weakly in her fist, and watched while the cornet—Blakeney—rewrapped Sherbourne's splint.

As she had not done then, Eleanor crouched at the head of the stretcher, and dropped a kiss upon Sherbourne's soaking forehead. The skin of his brow was so terribly cold that she drew away.

His face was changed. It was unscarred, unstubbled, with rounder cheeks and a chin more pointed. She knew the countenance, still, with its framing curls black and abundant; under her touch the beloved features were set and chill.

"Harry!"

She heard boots ringing near her, though all around was churned mud. Someone dragged at her, drawing her back from the body upon the stretcher, fighting back, hard, when Eleanor fought.

"Captain! Captain, at ease! I've no wish to hurt—*ow!*"

Eleanor's head was sore from a crack on the stillroom table, and all the room was pungent with brining herbs. Sherbourne stood over her, knocking blood off his lip.

"I own I thought you had seen the devil, woman."

"Beg pardon," said Eleanor, brushing lavender from him. "I was…not in myself."

"You as well, then?" asked Sherbourne. "Lucky bastards we. You might try drinking."

"Never," Eleanor shook her head.

"You have ruined it for the rest of us, giving Linton to lock my cellar. I much liked to hear you beg pardon for whaling me, though, just now." Sherbourne cleared his throat. "May I be of some help here? Harry is waking, and she asks for you."

SHE HAD LOST ALL the high, hectic color as the fever wore at her; a fortnight on, Harriet was pale as paper, but for the blue-gray smears beneath her eyes. The crisis would come by morning, Eleanor thought; or else it was arrived already—it had been easy to ignore with Harriet insensible and moaning. Now she half-sat on the pillows, possessed of near all her wit, and Eleanor had rather a carbine round in the chest. If the fever had slackened sufficient to lend back her mind, then in an hour, or three, it must spike or break. If it broke, then they might collect upon Sherbourne's promise, in a month or a year when Harriet's strength came back. If it rose, now, Harriet would not bear it, and Sherbourne must lay out for his last sister's coffin.

Harry knew.

"Sherry has just run out of here quite…as if the Black Gentleman stood by. Soon, I think—by morning—and I am sorry, Nora, if it does not go our way."

"Hold your apologies," said Eleanor, by way of greeting. "I want none."

"God keep you, madam," Harriet smiled, ghastly. "Ever a tender word for your beloved!"

She had brought feverfew and white willow up from the stillroom, and steeping them meant her hands must not lie idle; but she could not turn her tongue again to conversation, until Harriet shuddered and balked at the bitter drug.

"How have you forced that down me? I cannot!"

"Please," said Eleanor, all her fears distilled to a word. Harriet choked through it, half-retching, holding tight to Eleanor's hand. When half the cup was gone, Eleanor pressed no further.

"Nora, that is a murderous way to save one's life."

"Have it out of me in the morning."

"What, if only I live, you'll drink the rest of it?"

"If only you live," Eleanor nodded, and stroked stray droplets from Harriet's cheek.

"What must it feel like, do you think, to die?"

"Harry, this is morbid."

"So said Sherry, when I asked him, but he was not in the room when my sisters passed. They were not—not silly, as people think of women, but they were all so much afraid." Harriet held Eleanor's wrist, with surprising strength. "You have kept this watch by a hundred men. Why will you not do so, now, for me?"

"I do not think it needful."

"God, I had forgotten you and he were like to twins!"

Eleanor dug her thumbnail into her palm, and did not shout. "I will tell you my belief, though I nicked it from the Testament; *The last enemy that shall be destroyed is death.*"

Harriet gave the shadow of a laugh. "That must be comfort…for a soldier. Sherry has got it—"

"Inked upon his back, like any pirate. I forget, love, you are not always in search of one more fight." Eleanor sat in her shirt on the edge of the bed and untied her garters, as if it were one night among a thousand others. As if they were in her shabby house in London, and not the death-room of a country seat, she took what pillow Harriet would cede her, and gave over the lion's share of covers.

Harriet curled close to her as soon as she might, her head and hands afire on Eleanor's chest. Her eyes had half closed, and her mouth was open, to breathe; her voice came very small and dry. "Have I ever made bold and said so, Nora?"

"Said…?"

"I love you."

Harriet reached, when no answer came, to brush at Eleanor's cheek, and had the grace to say nothing more at all.

Eleanor had fallen asleep in a bed, with a blanket, and it was morning. There were birds—horrid birds—playing merry hob with her headache, but no other sounds; the pillows were perfect, the linen smooth and sweet with oil of roses. *Not a field hospital.* She ventured to stretch and open her eyes.

The bed's hangings were open, and through the windows the day promised fine. All Harriet's weight was against Eleanor's side, and her small, cool hand rested under Eleanor's shirt-front.

"Harry." Eleanor jerked upright, dousing them both from the cold cup of willow-bark by the bed. She came awake in a crash of candle-ends, tumblers, and distilling-pots. "Harry, Harry, please—"

Harriet croaked, without opening her eyes, "Christ. Stop *shouting*, Nora. Water?"

HARRIET MADE a good show of ignoring the riders, fiddling with *Melmoth the Wanderer* and the biscuits on the tea-tray beside her. Sherbourne did not dismount, only lifted his hat as he held the grey mare's rein, and hailed her with her Christian name; her brother's expression was a mix passing strange of discomfiture and pride. Fleming was half across the flagstones before she won Harriet's glance. Under a hussar's pelisse she was dressed too finely for riding; she had polished her Waterloo medal, and surely her boots had never rung so with her step before.

"Give you good evening, Harry. I hope you rested?"

"I had it from Linton this morning that you and Sherry had ridden hunting. A gentleman gives his staff *good* lies. My lord Captain, where have you been?"

Eleanor swept her hat to Harriet, half pleased, half contrite. "I have made my marriage allegation, madam."

Harriet took up the foolscap. It was much the color of her hand in the afternoon light, and Eleanor could still count all the fine bones. "Made oath in the consistory court…that he is a bachelor of an age of thirty-two years, and prayed a license… Oh, Nora."

"Dearest, what's the matter?"

"I never thought of it," said Harriet, dark brows bending. "This will bind you your whole life."

"That is rather the gist of a marriage-license."

"I meant, Nora," Harriet gestured over Eleanor's loose-cropped hair, her sabre and breeches. "You might have been free of—of *Nathaniel*, of all this; now you have gone and sworn to it. You should not have—not without consulting me."

"Do you not wish to be married?"

"Oh, I am not advanced enough in strength to grace that with an answer." Harriet rolled the paper and handed it to Eleanor with a smile. "Bend your head down."

Sherbourne turned his horse broadside when Eleanor obliged her, but did not look as he had in Thaxted Church that morning, when the archdeacon might have sown caltrops beneath his feet.

"I will take you as my mistress, if you like," Eleanor said when Harriet allowed her breath. "But Sherry has already perjured himself and paid for the paper. I beg you think of his convenience, if it troubles you."

Harriet laughed, a warm whisper of mirth just at Eleanor's ear. "You have ever been my comfort, Captain Fleming."

ABOUT THE AUTHOR

Jeannelle M. Ferreira is a poet, novelist, and lover of all things speculative, liminal, and numinous. She believes in ghosts, believes even harder in the internet, remains a flaming queer, and writes historical fiction because queer stories have always been there waiting in the margins. Her writing can be found in *Strange Horizons*, *The Moment of Change: An Anthology of Feminist Speculative Poetry*, *Queer Fish: Volume 2*, and *Steam-Powered 2: More Lesbian Steampunk Stories*. She enjoys period-accurate recipes and the NWHL, and lives in Maryland with her wife and daughter.

Made in the USA
Columbia, SC
29 March 2018